T0375717

Blood Oath

Michelle Lynn Tackes

iUniverse, Inc.
New York   Bloomington

iUniverse books may be ordered through booksellers or by contacting:

*iUniverse
1663 Liberty Drive
Bloomington, IN 47403
www.iuniverse.com
1-800-Authors (1-800-288-4677)*

*Because of the dynamic nature of the Internet, any Web addresses or
links contained in this book may have changed since publication and may
no longer be valid. The views expressed in this work are solely those of
the author and do not necessarily reflect the views of the publisher, and
the publisher hereby disclaims any responsibility for them.*

*ISBN: 978-1-4502-0098-1 (sc)
ISBN: 978-1-4502-0099-8 (ebook)*

Printed in the United States of America

iUniverse rev. date: 3/31/2010

I
A Brother's Love
Bucharest, Romania: 1871

As usual, the commotion surrounding the market-place was palpable. Every few feet there were magnificent wares to be sold; brilliantly colored tapestries, fine jewelry made of gold and silver and even Chrysolite, spices from around the world and fine silks. It was mid autumn, the busiest and best time of year for vendors, and their calls echoed to distant towns.

"Get your vegetables here!" called Regalus Heistad from his stand in the very heart of the city. "Get your vegetables, finest produce in the land! One week only! Lowest prices anywhere!" His call was loud and powerful, and filled with pride. He certainly had reason to be proud:

Heistad had farmed the land his entire life, working hard and reaping little, as had generations of his family before him. His farm had battled drought, floods, insect plagues and more. And yet he had managed to keep his family's livelihood going through it all. But now there was a war within the land, and business had not been good for him for many months.

"Good morrow, sir," the Parson called as he approached. "I will have one bushel of potatoes, one of leeks, and a kilogram of your best tobacco."

"Aye, very well." The aging farmer stooped and gathered the crops together, and the parson paid for them.

"How fares your family?" he asked companionably.

Heistad sighed a sigh of absolute exhaustion, and he suddenly looked much older than his fifty years. "I tell you, this war has made times meager indeed for us. The children are growing lean; it pains me to see them suffer so."

"I noticed that your son is not here. I daresay you could do with his help."

"He spends his days in the university now. Arania works twice as hard in the field as he does, and she is but ten years old."

"Don't judge him too harshly," The parson counseled. "He is but a boy, and a boy must learn to make his own way in the world."

"'Tis a dishonor to me, and to the land that gave him life. Speak not of it, for it makes me ill."

At that moment the courtyard outside the university was filling with students arrived for a lesson in medicinal herbs. Their general air of excitement was felt everywhere, as they chattered away with one another animatedly.

"Quiet, quiet, everyone," called the professor as he walked to the front of the room. "Now then, today we will be continuing our lesson on local herbs and their uses in medicine. Tell me, do any of you know what this herb is?" he asked, pointing to a low-growing, bushy plant with dark green, waxen leaves.

A handsome, olive-complected young man of eighteen who was standing near the front of the room raised a hand tentatively.

"Aye?"

"'Tis Marjoram," said the youth promptly, "'Tis usually to be found in shady areas with good soil and plenty of water."

"Aye," the professor said, approvingly. "Very good, Master Heistad. Can you tell me to what use it is put as a medicinal herb?"

"Marjoram is used in restorative draughts as a cough suppressant," Lysander Heistad rejoined. "It is usually supplemented with Tamarind and Fuganeek." His dark eyes were shining with enthusiasm.

"Yes, right again, Master Heistad. Now, who can identify this plant?" The professor indicated a star shaped red and gold tinged plant. "Miss Vendilan," he asked, looking to a willowy young woman to Lysander's left.

"That is Tamarind," said Graciela Vendilan, whose red hair was as fiery a color as the plant. "'Tis used to combat Hypothermia in a hot elixer and, like Lysander said, it is often used with Marjoram and Fuganeek to make a restorative drought."

"Aye." The professor grinned, pleased. "Yes, it is often possible to combine most plants to make more powerful elixirs and poultices suited to meet an patient's needs without adding superfluous ingredients. Tell me, what would you give someone who is feverish, in intense pain, and whose heart rate is erratic? But of course Master Heistad knows," he said, seeing Lysander's hand risen again and smiling.

"It seems to me," Lysander said promptly, "that such an individual is best treated with a combination of wild Mint for fever reduction, Lavender to alleviate their pain, and Chamomile or Wormwood to induce sleep and stabilize their pulse."

"Very good, very good. Study your herbs, for we will have an exam on the plants we have covered in a fortnight's time. Now then, let us set to work putting together the draught of which Lysander has just spoken. The herbs are located in the garden behind you, you shall need no more than an hour to find them, prepare them and steep them together in your kettles. And do not forget that a physician's timeliness will save his patient's life."

The students dispersed into the large, densely growing garden and began searching for the plants. Lysander was first to finish, collecting, chopping, and boiling his herbs within half an hour.

"Well done," the professor said when he was given the mixture, which was exactly the right color; deep gold. "Very well done, Lysander. This is a fine restorative draught." As the half hour became a whole, and the hour became two, he collected the work of the rest of the class.

"Very well done, everyone," he said at the end of the lesson. "We shall meet again in a week's time, and do not forget to study for that exam!"

The students gathered their things and departed. Lysander was collecting his phials of medicines together when the professor said, "Lysander, may I have a word with you?"

"Yes, professor?" The young man looked up curiously.

"You are my best student," the elderly physician said, "I have rarely ever seen such talent in healing. Dr. Barkoli is an old friend of mine, and he confided in me that he will need an assistant in his clinic. Tell, me, would you like to take the job? I would be more than happy to recommend you."

Lysander was silent for an interval of several moments. He would like nothing more than to work in the clinic. It would sharpen his skills, he loved to care for others, and he would be able to supplement his family's income. He had great respect for his father, but did not want to labor as an unskilled farmer as his father did. However, he knew that dishonoring one's parents was an offense punishable by death, and his father disapproved.

"I thank you most profoundly for your vote of confidence, Sir," he said cautiously. "I would like very much indeed to work in the clinic. But I must tell you, my father will not give me his consent."

"He disapproves?"

"Aye. I cannot go against his wishes. It is the supreme law of the land."

The elderly physician's face was solemn. "If that be the case, you must honor his wishes. I would advise you to try to persuade him, if you truly wish to continue your studies."

"Aye, that I will. Thank you, Professor." He put his vials in his bag and set off into the late October afternoon.

As he set off across the chilly courtyard, he spotted Graciela walking some paces ahead of him. "Hey, wait up!"

"I'm not slowing down," she called back playfully. "You hurry up!" So he did.

"I though I saw you out here. Must you listen at doors?" Lysander smiled at his friend and tucked his collar-length black hair behind his ears.

"Can I help it if I needed to get an extra vile for my fever reducing drought?" asked Graciela. "I promise, Lysander, I didn't hear anything. So what did the professor want to talk to you about anyway? If you don't mind me asking, that is," she added sarcastically.

"He asked me if I wanted to work in the clinic of one Dr. Barkoli. Apparently they're cohorts."

"Aye?" She looked at him with surprise, and also happiness. "That is wonderful. I work in the clinic myself, and I can tell you that you will never find a better doctor in Bucharest. Very knowledgeable and very kind."

"Is he? I've never met him, but the professor said he would be very pleased to recommend me. How long have you been working at the clinic? You never told me."

"You never asked," Graciela pointed out. "I have only been there for six months, but I love it."

"I thought you might say that," said Lysander. "I like what I'm hearing."

"So are you going to accept the offer?" Graciela asked.

"I would love to. I really would. But you know that children are not allowed to go against their parents' wishes. I've told you before that Papa will not let me do it, he was reluctant to let me study at the university to begin with."

Graciela actually stopped to stare at him, frowning. "Well, why not? You're the best in class, why shouldn't you be allowed to pursue your calling? It is an honor to have a son who can save lives."

Lysander sighed. "He believes it is a dishonor to him and the land. He thinks me selfish because I have left the land behind. I have great respect for Papa, but working in the fields day after day is not for me. I've no intention of being selfish, I fully intend to use my earnings to help him and Mother and Arania. Heaven only knows how long this war is to last."

"Then talk to him, "Graciela said surreptitiously. "That is your responsibility. You are not selfish, Lysander Heistad, and don't let anyone tell you different. You've as much right as anyone else to make your own way in the world."

"Aye, you are right. My family deserves better than a peasant's life. Arania has such confidence in me, `twould be a sore injustice to disappoint her." His ten-year-old sister was a remarkable creature. Frail and small with weak legs, she was nonetheless a happy, loving child who worked hard as a grown woman to help her family.

"I agree with you fully. I've wanted to ask, how is your sister? I've not seen her for some months."

"Busy as ever," Lysander said wearily. "I fear she might take ill soon, it's not safe for a young girl to be out in this weather. No doubt she'll be in the fields when I return home." Suddenly he stopped dead in his tracks and cried aloud, "Drat it all! I was supposed to assist with the harvest after lessons today."

"I'll see you next week!" Graciela called after him as he ran towards home.

When he entered his backyard through the whitewashed fence, he could see his sister hauling a large sack of beets up to the house to be packed for sale. She was struggling with both the weight of the sack and the cumbersome metal braces she wore on her legs. Even as he watched, she lost her balance and fell to the ground.

"Arania, don't take so many beets at once, you'll injure yourself." He went over to her and took the sack. "Here, let me help."

"Papa told us he needed all the beets ready to be sold by tonight," she said, already filling another sack that was nearly as large as the first. She sighed. "This is a much smaller harvest than last year's, I don't know if we'll have enough to break even."

"You worry too much," Lysander said, taking her hand to help her up. "Come on, Mama will be needing you in the house."

"Did you have a good lesson today, Lysander?"

"In fact I did," Lysander said, grinning as he remembered the days events. "Very interesting. But then, I enjoy every lesson. We were continuing the lesson from Monday on medicinal herbs, who would think that a little plant could mean the difference between life and death?"

"I know what you mean. `Tis amazing what the land can do, is it not?" Arania sighed. "Well, whatever happens, at least you have not been conscripted to serve in this war. I don't want to lose you, brother."

"You've nothing to fear," he said, putting an arm around her slim shoulders as they walked into the house. "I'm not going anywhere, I promise you that."

She laughed. "Good, because if we have another harvest like this, Papa just might go crazy."

"It's a wonder why he let me go to the university anyway."

"Because he knew you needed to find your own way," Arania said simply. "He did it because it was the best thing for you. He knows hoeing squash and potatoes isn't for you, even if he does not like it." She opened an empty crate and began packing the beets.

"Is that so?" He emptied out his own sack as well. "I was under the impression he thought it was a waste of time."

"He is only worried because of the troubles we have been having with the harvest. He is worried about providing for us all, and he knows no other means of living. He knows you care about us just as much as anyone. Change just frightens him."

"Maybe." He put the heavy wooden lid back on the crate. "But I wish he would trust me. I know how hard he works, and how worried he is about providing for us all."

"I know." Arania looked at him sadly. "I'm sorry that he seems to be so harsh on you. But he really does understand."

"Well, at least I know that one person thinks it's worthwhile," Lysander said, smiling at his sister. "That's all I was hoping to hear." Young though Arania was, she offered wise council, and he valued her opinions.

At that exact moment their mother entered from the front door, removing her shawl.

"Well, your father is in a lather," Helene Heistad said. "I hope you have a good explanation for being home late today, Lysander."

"When will Papa be getting home?" asked Arania.

"Very late. The postmaster delivered a letter today saying that there is a government order for twice the amount of tomatoes and cucumbers to be sent to the fighting troops. Without you to assist him he will be fortunate to arrive home before midnight."

"Sorry, Mama." Lysander looked at the ground. "But I really do have a good reason for it. I've had the most wonderful news."

"Aye? What is it, son?"

"My professor is friendly with Dr. Barkoli. He told me today that he is looking for new interns at his clinic and would be pleased to recommend me."

"Really? That's great!" Arania's face was jubilant, her gray-blue eyes were flashing with excitement.

"I am not sure this will end well," said Helene. "Your father is very worried. He is no longer young, and if you leave he will have to hire help for the upkeep of the shop. He cannot manage as much as he could before, you know, and it will not be easy to come by the funds to afford hired help."

"But Mama, I was intending to supplement his income with my earnings from the clinic. It will earn twice as much as what Papa does, and we could live better." He looked at his sister. "Do you not agree that Arania deserves to be able to walk without constantly being in pain? It could happen. All she would need is a simple procedure, and we could afford it."

"I do hate seeing her amble about in those braces."

"I don't want everyone to fuss over me," Arania said quietly. "I can get by. You and Papa need the money more than I do."

Lysander took his sister's small hand. "We can get by," he said gently. "We've managed to before. But you, you are a child who shoulders a grown woman's burden, and you do so gladly. I want to do this for you."

Arania's face drained of color, her eyes grew wide, and he knew she was frightened.

"Don't be afraid, Arania. Dr. Barkoli is an excellent surgeon. He won't let anything happen to you. I won't let anything happen to you."

"You are sure?"

"Trust me," he reassured her. "I wouldn't suggest anything that was not in your best interest. I'm your brother."

Arania sighed.

"'Tis a most generous offer, Lysander," their mother said. She looked over at her daughter. "What say you, my dear girl? Would you not like to be stronger?"

Arania did not respond immediately: her eyes were narrowed, deep in thought. Finally she said carefully, "Aye. The idea of the procedure still frightens me, but my desire to be a better help to my family is stronger than any fear."

"I'll stay with you the whole time," Lysander promised her. "Everything will be fine."

The fear immediately left Arania's face. Her brother could cheer her like no one else could, and she trusted him completely.

"Thank you, Lysander."

They ate diner, the siblings helped their mother to wash the dishes, and after they had packed the rest of the beets it was time for Arania to go to bed. The rickety, splintery staircase was dangerous for anyone, let alone a frail little girl, so Lysander carried her up-small as she was it was no difficulty for him.

"We need to repair these staircases," he said frowning down at them. "Here we are." He went into her small room and set her carefully on the bed, then helped her to remove the braces.

Suddenly he stopped. "Arania!" There were red marks and cuts all over her legs.

"The braces do it," she said, looking at the cuts without concern. He, on the other hand, was very concerned.

"Why didn't you tell us? Do Mama and Papa know?"

"Nay. It's nothing, just some small cuts."

"Arania, 'tis very important that you tell us if these braces are injuring you, very, very important, do you understand? Cuts like these can become infected very easily; they can make you very ill."

She nodded solemnly.

"Well," he said slowly, looking at the lacerations once more, "these don't appear to be infected, thank the Lord. I'll get some salve for them. But, Arania, you've got to tell us about these kinds of things so we can help you."

He left and returned with a healing salve which he spread carefully over the cuts, then bound them with woven bandages so they would stay protected. Silence elapsed for several moments.

"I- I didn't want to be a bother to anyone," his sister said falteringly. "Mama and Papa have so much on their minds as it is." She looked up at him. "Are you angry?"

At first Lysander did not reply, he merely kept his eyes on his work. His face was impassive, but when he spoke his voice was gentle.

"No," he said. "No, not angry. The only bother is these infernal contraptions. I don't know why I didn't think of getting you that procedure before; it should have been done ages ago." He finished binding the wounds and stood carefully. "Do you feel all right?"

She nodded. "Yes, thank you, Lysander."

"I don't care what Papa says." He pulled the blankets up around her, and his face wore a determined set. "First thing in the morning I'm going to speak to Dr. Barkoli about that position. I'm going to make sure you get the help you need."

"No!" she gasped suddenly. "You can't disobey Papa. You know it's punishable by death."

"Then that is a death I will be proud to suffer." Smiling, he leaned over and kissed her on the forehead gently. "Good night, my love."

"Good night." She was soon asleep, and he went to his own room, smiling.

The next day he went to the clinic and submitted his recommendation.

"Very good. Aye, very good indeed." The elderly physician read through the papers with satisfaction. "You have taken intermediate and advanced courses in medicinal herbs and surgical procedures, have placed highest in your class, and have interned through the university. Well then, your responsibilities will be to document update the register and room patients when they arrive. You will be advanced after a six month supervisory period and obtaining a 90% on a mastery exam."

"I will be pleased to assist in any way dictated to me," Lysander said humbly. "Sir, I have a request of my own to make: I hope it will not sound impertinent, but it is quite important."

"Aye?"

"I have a sister, you see. She is a frail little thing with weak legs and is conscribed to wearing cumbersome braces. `Tis most painful for her. I had hoped that she might have this ailment corrected."

"`Tis a simple enough procedure," agreed the doctor. "I regret to say that we are incredibly busy at this time, but `tis wiser all the same that you wait until you have been paid. Bring the child round next week, and I will examine her then to determine if she is a suitable candidate for the surgery."

"Aye. Thank you, sir. This will mean so much to her."

"I am glad to help."

Lysander went home and helped his mother and sister with the chores. As it was a Saturday, they finished at six p.m., and after dinner brother and sister both went into the forest to collect herbs, as it was a past time enjoyed by both siblings.

"Oh look, this is Tamarind, isn't it? The stuff used to fight hypothermia?" She knelt down beside the star-shaped plants and grabbed a handful. "And this is

Chamomile, is it not?" She also collected a handful of the stubby little plants with white blossoms.

"Aye. We use that to induce sleep."

"You mean like when someone is in pain?"

"Aye," he said, nodding. "'Tis kinder than to keep them awake sometimes." He watched her stand and stow the herbs in her carrying pouch.

"So you went to the clinic to ask about the open post, didn't you? Did you get hired?"

"Yes. Arania, I talked with Dr. Barkoli about you. He wants you to come in next week for an examination to see if you are a suitable candidate for the procedure."

"I hope I am," she said gloomily. "Maybe then everyone at school wouldn't see me as such a freak." Arania attended the local grammar school. While she was one of the best students, the others often antagonized her because of the braces on her legs. Yet another reason for her to go through with the procedure, he thought.

He put an arm around her shoulders. "Arania Leila Heistad, don't ever let me hear you talk about yourself that way again. You are not a freak, and anyone who says differently is a liar."

She grinned wanly at him. "I bet you have never been heckled, have you?"

At this her brother laughed out loud. "I'm the best in my class. Of course I have."

Arania shook her head as she moved on to another patch of land. "Marjoram. This is the one used to stop bleeding, isn't it?"

"Aye. Very good." He grinned as he watched her add this to her pouch also, and wondered fleetingly if she might chose to become an apothecary herself when she was grown. She was certainly a quick enough learner, and so caring and compassionate. Exactly the type of person who would be perfectly suited for such work.

She turned slowly to him now and asked, carefully, "Lysander? Will this be a painful procedure?" Some of the concern was back in her eyes.

"Nay. Dr. Barkoli will put you to sleep before he begins his work. You won't feel a thing."

"That`s a relief." Grinning, she went over to some bright green plants with miniscule purple flowers. "Oh, here's Lavender. I think I remember you saying this reduces pain. And Thyme, which protects you from infection." She also added these to her pouch.

"Very good." He helped her to her feet. All of a sudden both siblings heard a loud, angry growl which they knew to be that of a hungry wolf.

"Arania, come, now!" He grabbed her hand and started running. Arania did her best to keep up with him, but she simply could not run as quickly or as easily as he could, and she screamed as she tripped over a raised tree root. Her hand was wrenched from her brother's, and she fell down a ravine and out of sight.

"Arania! Arania!" He ran down the steep grade, and what he saw at the bottom nearly stopped his heart with fear. His precious little sister was lying unconscious at the foot of the hill, and the wolf was coming closer to her.

Abandoning all concern for his own safety, he charged at the animal, brandishing his knife. "Get away! Get away from her! Leave her alone!" The beast growled angrily, but thought better of tangling with him. It snarled once more, and then left.

Breathing hard, Lysander turned his attention back to his sister. "Arania. Arania, wake up." He shook her shoulder gently, but she merely gave a groan of pain, and her eyes opened for a brief second before closing again.

What is wrong with her? He wondered. Looking down, he saw that her right leg was tangled in a bush of briars. He carefully cut her loose, and as he did so, he noticed the bleeding snakebite on her ankle.

"Hold on." Fighting down his own fear, he used his candle to start a fire, and then set to work preparing a poultice of Globe Mallow Root and Thyme leaves. He dipped his handkerchief into the clean water of his canteen and used it to clean the wound, then applied the poultice to draw out the venom when it was ready.

Papa is right, he thought gloomily, *I am selfish, and here is final proof. How could I have put someone I love so much into such danger? She'll never forgive me.*

Lysander remained by his sisters side all though the night, monitoring her pulse, listening to her shallow respiration, praying that she would awaken. Finally, late the next morning, she opened her eyes and looked up at him.

"Lysander?"

"I'm here," he said gently. He put a hand to her forehead; she was still a bit feverish, though less so than she had been in the night. "You're going to be all right. Just relax."

"Have we been out here all night?" she asked.

"Yes. You've been ill, a snake bit you when you fell into the ravine, but I've drawn out the venom and cleaned the wound." He sighed. "I am so sorry, Arania, I wasn't thinking."

"Don't be ridiculous." Arania grinned weakly and placed her small hand inside his. "Lysander-I owe you my life."

He squeezed back. "You owe me nothing."

Just then the siblings heard their father's fearful shout. "Arania! Lysander!" Had he been looking for them all night?

He was coming closer. *"Arania! Lysander!"*

"Here we are, Papa," Lysander said. In a few moments Regalus Heistad was striding up to them with their mother behind him.

Helene Heistad gasped aloud. "Arania!" she cried out. "Good heavens, child, what has happened to you?"

"A wolf attacked us," Lysander said. "She fell down the ravine when we were running away, and a snake bit her, I couldn't move her."

"She *what?!*" Regalus` face was red with anger. "Lysander Nigelus Heistad, how could you have let this happen to your little sister? You are supposed to take care of her!"

"I've treated the wound. She'll be fine, she just needs to rest." Even as he said it Lysander knew his argument would do no good at all.

"All you have done, boy," his father snarled, "is covered up your selfishness, and by doing so proven just how selfish you are! No doubt this came of you attending that university, it seemed a bad idea to me from the start."

"Regalus, calm yourself," Helene consoled. "He has taken responsibility for his mistake."

"That is immaterial!" roared Regalus. "For Heaven's sake, Helene, she could have died! The boy must realize this! He knows she can't run like he can, he should have never brought her here to begin with! And what for? To look for stupid plants, I have never heard of anything so foolish."

"Those foolish plants saved my life," spoke up Arania, "And my brother is not selfish. You go too far, Papa!" Her gray-blue eyes were fiery, and there was a hard anger in her voice that was hardly ever heard.

"Arania!" her mother gasped.

"Calm yourself, you need to rest," her brother implored her.

She kept her eyes fixed on her father as she continued firmly, "It wasn't Lysander's fault I fell, he was trying to protect me from the wolf. He should be allowed to pursue his calling."

"His calling?" Regalus asked.

"Yes, calling. He stayed with me all night taking care of me, and he was amazing. You would know that if you had been here."

"She-she is right," Helene agreed tentatively.

"You misunderstand me, Papa," said Lysander, standing with Arania in his arms. "Farming the land is not for me. But that does not mean I care nothing for my family. You three will always be my topmost priority, and you will always have me to depend on."

Regalus remained silent, thinking everything over.

"I have been offered an internship in Dr. Barkoli`s clinic," his son said tentatively. "If you will give me your approval, Papa, I would very much like to accept the offer."

All eyes were on Regalus waiting for his answer; he seemed incapable of speech.

"You may accept," he finally said, in a somewhat grudging manner.

"I won't forget my word. Thank you, father. Now then, we need to get Arania home so she can rest comfortably."

Regalus looked concernedly at his little daughter. "Are you quite sure you feel all right, my dear?"

"Aye. Lysander spoke the truth. I'll be back on my feet soon."

So the family went home. "I can hardly believe it," Arania said as Lysander took her up to her room and laid her on the bed carefully. "Well done, Lysander."

"I owe it all to you," he said, removing her braces. "That took courage on your part."

Arania grinned nonchalantly. "You owe me nothing. This is the way it's supposed to be."

"The world doesn't always work the way it ought to," her brother said with grim satisfaction. He pulled the blankets around her. "Let yourself recuperate, my dear, I will see to today's chores. I'm right here if you need me."

Arania nodded woozily and was soon asleep again.

Arania took a full day to recover completely from her ordeal. Nevertheless, she was at the clinic the following week for her examination, as scheduled. For half an hour she sat with Lysander in the waiting area, silent and pale as a ghost.

Sensing her uneasiness, Lysander took her hand and smiled encouragingly. She could not help but return the grin, although there was still a trace of fright in her delicate features. She would grow into a very beautiful young woman one day, he thought.

"Arania Heistad?" Dr. Barkoli had emerged from the exam room, ready for her. She stood and, trying with all her might not to tremble, walked over to the elderly physician with her brother behind her.

"Hello, my dear," he said kindly. "Your brother has told me much about you. Now if you will please follow me-there's no reason to be nervous-this way."

In the exam room Dr. Barkoli began by asking Arania some questions.

"How old are you, Arania?"

"Ten years."

"And how long have you worn these braces on your legs?"

"Always. My last physician said the bones in my ankles don't align properly."

"Do these braces ever hurt you in some way? Do they leave cuts or marks?"

"Yes." This time it was not Arania who answered, but Lysander. "I noticed a great many cuts on her legs a few days ago."

"So I see. Arania, I'm going to take these braces off and examine the bone alignment in your ankles, all right? It might not be possible to repair them by surgery, you understand."

She nodded solemnly. He carefully removed the braces, observed the lacerations on her legs, and then gently touched her ankles, feeling the delicate bones beneath her olive skin.

"Well, young lady, we will certainly be able to correct this, and I say the sooner you can walk without these braces, the better. Cuts like these are very dangerous."

She nodded.

"Fortunately none of these have become infected. You must keep a close eye on them to ensure that they heal."

"Aye, so we will," Lysander agreed.

"Has she any dysfunctions of the lungs?" The doctor asked him. "We must determine if she is strong enough to survive being anesthetized."

"She is prone to illness in the colder weather," was the reply, "but aside from that I cannot think of anything."

"Very well, `twill be noted that she is to be kept warm while the procedure is in progress. But it will not be a serious impediment.

Now then, the wounds on her legs must heal completely before the surgery can be done, so as to reduce the risk of infection; a fortnight's time ought be sufficient. She will need to remain in the hospital afterwards because it takes two month's time to recuperate fully from the surgery, and I shall need to monitor her progress to ensure she is healing properly."

"Very well." Lysander hugged his sister. "I will have to speak with my father, but I am sure he will see the merit of sparing her further pain."

Lysander spoke with his parents that evening, and both Regalus and Helene agreed that it would be best for Arania to undergo the surgery. Lysander spent the next two weeks working hard both in the fields and in the clinic, and by the time his sister was due to go into the hospital he had been able to pay for her procedure in full, with help from his parents.

Early on the morning of the surgery an assistant took Arania's pulse, listened to her breathing and looked at the size of her pupils, then documented the information in a scroll.

"Very well, everything seems to be in order," she said, closing the scroll. "The doctor will come in a few minutes to administer the anesthetic." Smiling at Arania, she left.

Silence reigned for several moments. Then Arania asked, "Where are Mama and Papa? They said they would be here by this morning." Arania had been in the hospital since the night before: She had bathed and was dressed for the surgery in a plain shift, but she was not ready to be anesthetized. Her brother could see it in her eyes.

"Mama and Papa sent me a telegram last night," he said gently, "While you were sleeping. They needed to stay at the shop; the new order has just arrived. No, don't cry," he added quickly, because tears were falling down her face. "They can't help it, don't be angry with them. They'll be here when you wake up, I promise. And I'll be here, too. I won't leave you." He hugged her, and slowly her grief subsided.

Just then Dr. Barkoli entered. "Ah, Miss Arania. How are you?"

She took a deep breath and looked at her brother. "I'm well."

"Here, drink this," he said, handing her a paper cup. She began to drink, and then stopped suddenly.

"I-I feel so strange," she murmured faintly. Her eyes were heavy, and she swayed slightly on the bed.

"An Infusion of Thyme and Wormwood," The doctor explained to Lysander. "She will need a strong sleeping draught; I have also added Asphodel to relax her." He put his hands on Arania's shoulders and carefully laid his young patient back on the pillow, then dipped a rag into a small bowl of Chloroform and put this to her forehead. The contact of the cold liquid to her skin made her gasp aloud, even in her incapacitated state.

"Shh. Just breathe, everything will be fine. Don't worry." She breathed deeply of the Chloroform fumes, and in moments she was in a deep sleep where she could feel no pain.

"You could do with a sleeping draught yourself, son," Dr. Barkoli said, looking now to Lysander as he pulled a warm blanket over her. "You look well done in."

Lysander kept his eyes on his helpless sister. He did not want to leave her for even a moment; he knew there was every chance that she might never awaken. Surgeries were so dangerous.

"You can stay in the waiting area," The doctor said. "Get some sleep; we'll notify you when she has been moved to recovery. She will be safe."

Lysander did not like this idea, but he was exhausted from working so hard to finance the procedure. Besides, he knew he would not be allowed to stay with his sister while the operation was in progress. He gave her limp hand one last squeeze, whispered, "I love you, Arania," and then walked to the waiting area.

Well, at least I'm nearby, he thought as he sat down. *It's better than nothing.* He looked out the window into the fall sunshine and was soon asleep.

He was awakened some five hours later by a gentle hand on his shoulder. Looking up, he saw that it was his mother who had roused him. Standing a bit to her right was his father, and both looked extremely worried.

He stood up. "Mama, Papa, when did you get here?"

"Scarcely more than five minutes ago," said his mother.

"We have not heard any news of your sister as yet, we are very concerned."

"I must go to her," Lysander said, standing up. "I promised I would be there when she wakes up."

"No, you must wait for the doctor's permission. She is still very weak."

Just then Dr. Barkoli arrived from the recovery room.

"Good Morrow, you must be Arania's parents."

"Aye," Regalus said, stepping forward. "Regalus Heistad. This is my wife, Helene; I believe you know my son?"

"Aye, Lysander works in my clinic." He turned to the youth. "Your sister gave us a real fright when we were stitching her up, her pulse plummeted. We nearly lost her."

"Is she all right?" Lysander asked, cutting to the essentials.

"I pray that she will be, but we haven't been able to wake her yet."

This was just what Lysander had been dreading, but he struggled to keep his voice calm when he asked, "Where is she?"

"Through there," said his employer with a sigh, indicating a small room just off the main operating theatre, "But I warn you, she is in rough shape, lad."

"I need to see her," Lysander insisted, and he went into the room with his parents and the physician in his wake.

Arania lay sleeping on a cot next to the window. Beneath the blankets, Lysander knew that rows of black stitches closed the surgical wounds on her legs, which were splinted to keep the bones in their proper alignment as they healed, and yet she seemed to be at peace in her slumber. A young surgeon, one of his colleagues, sat at her side, listening to her heartbeat. Seeing the family approach, he stood up and replaced the stethoscope around his neck.

"Has there been any change?" Dr. Barkoli asked.

The young surgeon shook his head. "No, nothing. Her vital signs are normal, but she's still in as deep a sleep as ever." He frowned. "I don't understand it."

His employer also frowned. "Well, perhaps we used too strong an anesthetic. She is very delicate."

Lysander knelt at his sister's bedside and took her small hand. It was cold, and yet he could feel life thrumming in her veins as surely as anything. He massaged the little hand in his own, trying to think what he could do....perhaps she just needed to know he was there, as he had said he would be....yes....

Suddenly, to the astonishment of the onlookers, he gave the tiniest of smiles. "I can wake her." He leaned over and kissed Arania on the forehead, and sure enough, her eyes fluttered open.

"Lysander. I thought I heard your voice." She reached for him, and he enveloped her in a gentle hug.

"I'm here, darling."

"Mama," Arania said now, and reached for her mother, who let out a cry of joy.

"Oh, my precious little child," Helene Heistad exclaimed, and rushed forward to embrace her daughter. Regalus, too, hugged her.

"We are most grateful to you for looking after our little Arania," he said to the physicians, shaking hands with each in turn. "We feared for her life."

"It was a pleasure," said Dr. Barkoli. He knelt down at Arania's eye level. "How are you feeling, my dear?"

"Sore," was the reply, "but glad to have my brother with me."

The physician handed her another cup of medicine with a sweet scent to it. "Here, this will ease the pain."

She began to drink. "Slowly, child, or it won't work properly," he cautioned.

Arania finished the concoction slowly, and then said, "I knew you would be here for me, Lysander."

Lysander stroked his sister's silken black hair. "I love you, Arania," he said softly, "More than anything."

Lysander was kept very busy at his new job, but he went to see Arania in the hospital whenever he could.

"How much longer before I can come home?" Arania asked one night in early December.

"A few more weeks," Lysander answered, smiling. "How impatient you are." He knew this was difficult for her. She was used to working, not staying in bed, and it was lonely without anyone she knew to keep her company. But she was less restless when he was near her.

"I just can't help thinking about Mama and Papa. Snow is falling fast on us, and they won't keep warm without enough hands to get the work done."

"I'm helping out as often as I can, and they have hired extra help." He sat in the chair beside her cot. "You'll make yourself ill with all this worry, Arania, and then `twill be even longer before you can leave. Mama and Papa are eager to have you back home."

"I miss them so." Regalus and Helene had been able to come up only once, they had been incredibly busy. "Dr. Barkoli is very kind, though."

"Aye, he is. I told you that you would be well cared for." He could see the relief coming into her face. "I know how you feel, Arania. But he says you're getting stronger every day. Try to be patient; you'll be home before you know it."

"I'll try." She sighed.

"I've brought you an early Christmas gift," he said, pulling a book out from his coat pocket and handing it to her. After all, she would not be home before the month was out, and he did not know if he would be able to see her before then.

She beamed at her brother. "Oh, thank you, Lysander." It was the third in a series of books that were the most well-known in the land. A tale that went back two thousand years, that told of forbidden love between a wealthy young sorcerer named Amadyn and his uncle's beautiful young maidservant, Mariela. Arania had heard about it from other children in her grammar school, but had never read a copy of the story herself.

He grinned back. "Happy Christmas, my love."

She flipped through the book. "One feels a sense of pity for Amadyn, doesn't one? It was awful for them to prosecute him because of what he could do."

"Well, he didn't exactly exercise a lot of self control, did he?" Lysander was also looking at the book. "He sometimes couldn't even look at people without hypnotizing them, nearly killed some of them."

"But it wasn't his fault. He couldn't control it. No more than you can help being good at healing people. It was wrong, just like it was wrong for Papa to call you selfish."

"It makes me glad that he had a few happy years at least." She stopped at a point near the end of the book and began to read. "He really loved Mariela, didn't he?"

"Aye. He didn't have much else. It isn't so surprising that he reacted the way he did to her death."

"No. But that doesn't make it right. Leaving his infant son all alone to die. I would hope that if I died before my time, you would look after Mama and Papa for me." Her eyes were wide and solemn. "They will not always be able to keep up the shop like they do now, you know."

"Don't talk like that, Arania," Lysander said. "You won't be leaving this world for a very long time to come."

"He didn't deserve to be killed by that vampire, though. How painful and frightening it must be."

"Aye. I've read that their bite is like a horrible burn. But you know there are no such things as vampires, don't you?"

"Yes, I know. Thank God for that." She shuddered.

"Arania, what's wrong?" He looked at her with concern. "Are you chilled?"

"No. It's nothing, I'm fine." But Arania didn't feel fine. If she hadn`t known better, she would have sworn something evil was watching her that very moment.

"It's late," Lysander said, looking at the clock above the wall. "I should be going, you should get some sleep." He bent down and hugged Arania. "I'll see you when you come home, all right?"

"All right." She grinned. After all, there was no safer place for her to be than a hospital, was there? She had no reason to fear.

"I`ll come back to see you again as soon as I can. Rest easy, my love." And he left.

On his way out he ran into Graciela. "What are you doing here?"

"Working," she said, brushing lint off of her orderly uniform. "I talked with Dr. Barkoli about it, and we arranged for me to take Mondays and Tuesdays here, and the rest of the week at the clinic. You're here visiting Arania, aren't you?"

"Aye. I can't come often enough."

"Is Arania well? Dr. Barkoli is taking care of her, is he not?"

"Aye. She's well. `Tis difficult for her to be away from home for so long, though. She worries for our parents. No doubt being forced to remain in bed is irritating her something fierce."

"You did the right thing by getting her that surgery," Graciela said. "She doesn't deserve to be in pain constantly. No child does."

"I know. She's going to be fine, I've no doubt of that."

"She really is extraordinarily lucky. A child could not hope to have a better sibling than you, and a hospital could not hope to have a better physician."

"I don't understand. What do you mean?"

"Don't tell me you don't know when it is obvious to me." She grinned at him. "We have known each other ever since we both came to the university, after all."

"If you're saying this because of my class rank, there are far more important things to be than clever. And I wouldn't even be so quick to classify myself as that." He sighed. "Arania nearly died because of me once. I knew she couldn't run well, and yet I pressured her to fly. My father was absolutely furious."

"The way I heard it, you saved her life. The wolf would have torn her to bits if you hadn't been there, and you saved her when she was bitten by that snake. I say these things because you are kind and compassionate, which is more than can be said for plenty of other men."

"But don't you see? That's not the point. I shouldn't have taken her out there in the first place, it is too dangerous for a little girl. It wasn't compassion to put her in danger, it was thoughtlessness."

"You took her out there because she asked you to. The earth gives both of you the same joy. She looks up to you and loves you endlessly, and you would do anything to keep her from harm." She stopped and turned to look at him full on. "You see, it is your empathy that will make you a great physician, not cleverness. You need a bond of trust in order to treat someone effectively, and trust is not gained through cleverness alone. Plenty of the smartest ones don't know that."

"It will be so good to have her home again. She almost didn't survive the procedure."

She gasped aloud. "You never told me that."

"I didn't want to alarm you." He put an arm around her shoulders. "You know, it's not so surprising that you two get on so well. You would both take on the cares of the world in a second, and never mind what it meant for you." He laughed. "Maybe that's why we get on so well."

"Do you speak the truth?" she asked, looking quizzically at him. "Oh, Lysander."

He grinned. "Have you ever known me to be false?"

Lysander was not able to visit his sister in the hospital again, but Graciela happily went in his stead whenever she was working there. Finally, five days into the New Year, Arania was strong enough to go home. Lysander could not remember such a joyous day, his mother was weeping for happiness.

"You see?" Lysander said to her as he helped her into bed that night-she would be walking with a walking stick for another week until her balance came back. "I told you that you would be home before you knew it."

"And so I am now," She hugged him. "Thank you for being there; you have been an indescribable comfort to me."

He grinned. "Anytime, dear sister. Rest easy."

II
The Last Promise
December, 1875

Arania entered the small house grinning from ear to ear. "Mama, wonderful news. We have received an invitation to the Yule Ball at the Imperial Palace in a fortnight's time." Her face was a bright pink, and her eyes were shining.

"How fun 'twill be," Helene said, putting an arm around her daughter's shoulders. "It has been such a long time since we have had the time for celebration."

"Who sent the invitation?" Lysander asked, looking at the piece of paper in the girls hand. "Who is the host?"

She looked at the invitation. "'Tis from Dr. Barkoli. Now, why would he invite one of his patients to a social event?" She frowned.

"You wouldn't be going as that, you would be a guest. Besides, if anyone deserves a night of relaxation and merriment, it's you, Arania." Lysander took the invitation from her. "Don't give his title another thought. If he does speak of you, 'twill be to admire the beautiful young lady you are becoming." Arania was fourteen years old now, and had indeed turned out to be as fair of face on the outside as she was kind on the inside. Willowy and slender with big, brilliant eyes and a smile that could light up a room, she had recently been courted by Hyman Arevrel, a stately youth who attended her school.

Arania laughed. "Oh, go on."

"You will need a new dress for such an occasion," Helene said. Arania was not a vain girl, and had never thought of such luxuries as silks. There had been too much work to be done, and not enough money. But things had been a bit better for the family as of late.

"I agree," Lysander said, grinning. "This is an occasion that calls for finery."

"And will Papa be going, too?"

"Nay, he has no liking for such affairs. He will not mind."

"Aye. I see." Arania picked up a bucket. "I should be going; the cows will need to be fed before dark."

"Wait, I will help you," Lysander said. "'Tis not wise for a young girl to be out in this cold for long. There have been outbreaks of Typhoid Fever in the town, don't forget."

"I won't forget," Arania said, grinning, and she headed out the door with her brother following.

In the small barn Arania poured the feed into the trough while Lysander mucked out their stalls. It was already nearly twilight, and a fierce wind was howling. The newborn calf lowed anxiously.

"Don't be so frightened, small one," Arania said, and she patted its furry hide. The young beast fell silent and leaned its head over so she could scratch behind its ears. Smiling, Arania began to sing to the calf.

"Tomorrow there will be a new day arriving,
And there will be a chance to keep trying
So cry no more, my little precious one
Just look into the wonder of the noonday sun
The strength of the mountains never fades away
And so will my love forever be the same."

Lysander listened to his sisters sweet voice as he looked out on the snow covered land. Ordinarily the calf would be absolutely terrified of such a windstorm as this, but with Arania there it was completely content. She had a gift for empathy.

Just then they heard the wagon coming up the path, and Arania ran out into the frigid eve to greet their father, faster than would have ever been possible four years previously, followed by Lysander.

"Papa! Papa!"

Regalus was nearly to the front door when his children reached him. Laughing, he caught Arania in his arms and hugged her tightly.

"Good morrow, my child," he said happily. "I say, you are the merriest looking sprite I have ever beheld. Your cheeks are red as apples."

"'Tis a merry time of year."

"Aye. This will be a comfortable winter with the profits we have had. Where is your mother?"

"In the house. She is making dinner, and we have seen to the cows."

"Good girl. Let us go inside quickly, this cold bites into my bones."

The three of them went in to the house where Helene was preparing hot soup on the woodstove. "Here, Arania," she said, filling a bowl for her daughter as they took their places at the table.

The girl took it with thanks, then turned to her father and said, "Papa, we have had some exiting news today."

"Aye?"

"We have received an invitation to the Imperial palace for a Yule ball on the thirty-first," she specified. "Dr. Barkoli is the host; he has invited his employees and their families."

"An honor indeed," Regalus said, fixing his son with a look that held much more pride than the youth had seen of late. Lysander smiled back, just slightly. "I should hope that you will attend?"

"Of course. Arania, too."

"If you will permit me to do so," said Arania, humbly, looking down at her bowl.

"I see no problem with that," Regalus said, "So long as you will be with your brother." He looked to Lysander. "You shall return home by nine o'clock, no later. A young girl needs her rest."

"Very well," said both siblings in tandem.

They finished their dinner and then Arania helped her mother wash and dry the dishes, and Lysander helped his father stock fresh hay in the barn before he left to return to his own small home on the other end of town. The wind was still raging, but he felt happy.

The next day Lysander had the afternoon off from work, so when Graciela asked him if he would fancy a walk down to the village markets, he happily agreed.

They walked past vendors selling Christmas roses and sticks of incense which left trails of colored smoke in the cold air behind them, past bookshops and clothing shops, without a care in the world except where to stop first. Christmas day was in less than a week, and Graciela still needed to find gifts for her family.

"What do you think of this one?" she asked, holding up a beautiful wreath of poinsettias. "It will make a lovely accent for the doorpost, will it not?"

"Aye," he agreed. "Your family must be very excited to have you home this week."

"And yours to have you home, as well." She turned to another shelf and picked up a gold-leafed copy of Amadyn the Magician.

"Wonderful tale, isn't it?" she said, flipping through the pages. "I've never read it myself, but Arania recounted it to me once."Graciela sighed. "You are very lucky to have such a fine girl for a sister."

"I know it," he said, with a smile. "'Tis good that she has the ball to look forward to."

"She is going?" Graciela asked. "Aye, I might have known. With Hyman Arevrel, no doubt?"

"Aye. She is most exited, 'tis a pleasure to see. She will need a new dress, though, she has only homespun shifts."

He stopped to look into the window of a shop that sold silks and satins in every color and pattern imaginable. One bolt of fabric caught his eye in particular: a fiery red that would complement Arania's dark hair and warm skin perfectly.

"How fine she would look in red," he said to himself. Unfortunately, this shop was rather expensive, and Lysander could not afford fabric at those prices. He sighed.

"Oh, that reminds me," said Graciela, rummaging into her satchel, "I have a present for Arania." She produced a package wrapped in brown paper and handed it to him. Carefully he unwrapped it, and found a dress in exactly his sister's size, made of fine red silk.

At first he was speechless. It was perfect, absolutely perfect! Finally he managed to say, "Graciela-how did you ever afford this? It must have cost a fortune!"

"Oh, I didn't buy it." She grinned magnificently. "My mother spun it; she can work miracles with a spindle." Graciela slid an arm around his waist. "I thought Arania might need a new dress for her special night."

He returned her embrace enthusiastically. "Thank you, Graciela, thank you from the both of us. She's going to love it."

"It was no trouble."

"Tell me, are you planning to go to the ball? I daresay that you have received an invitation."

"Aye. But I have no one to go with." She frowned.

"Well, I would be honored to go with you."

"Aye?" She beamed at him. "Very well, then."

Just then they heard the grandfather clock in the middle of the square chime noon.

"Oh, damn," Lysander muttered, "I told Papa I would return the borrowed tinderbox to the silversmith's by two."

He turned onto the next street and began the long walk home. Even on days like this his responsibilities never ended.

One week later it was Christmas day. Lysander went to his parents' house for breakfast, and then the family went to church together. Arania was in the children's Sunday school choir, who gave a performance after the service. She herself sang the last song as a solo, and the small citadel rang with applause.

"You were terrific," Lysander said, putting an arm around his sister's shoulders as the family walked home that afternoon. "I was so proud."

"`Twas nothing," she replied, a delicate pink suffusing her face. Despite the cold he noticed that she was perspiring, and looked quite tired. It worried him.

She, however, seemed to be thinking about anything but the cold. She raised her face to the sky in the midst of a light snowfall, grinning from one ear to the other, and held out a hand to catch the flakes. "I feel like Heaven is showering us with diamonds. `Tis a blessing to be alive on a day like this."

"Aye." Helene smiled at her. "`Tis a blessing indeed that we are all alive and well."

Lysander stooped and hoisted Arania onto his shoulders, the way he used to when she still wore her braces. "Go on, Arania, catch the blessings. They will keep you safe in the new year."

Laughing out loud, Arania held out both hands to catch the pristine little flakes while her brother held her steady on his shoulders.

"Blessings for Mama," she said happily, "And for Papa, and for my dear older brother. As long as I have the three of them, there is no one in the world luckier than me."

Lysander laughed. "We are just as lucky."

They finally reached the small house and hurried inside where they sat by the fireplace with mugs of hot chocolate, reading aloud from a book of Christmas stories. A storm blew up over the course of the afternoon, but the family was safe and comfortable in the house, quite enjoying themselves.

At seven that evening Helene called them in for dinner, and they devoured a feast of roast turkey, corn, potatoes, and rhubarb pie for dessert. Then it was time to open the gifts. There were few, and very soon they had all been opened.

Then Lysander suddenly remembered the package from Graciela. "Arania, this reminds me, I have one more gift for you." He walked over to the tree and picked up the very last package, the light lump wrapped in brown paper he had concealed from view. He handed it to his sister.

"Here. This is from both me and Graciela as well."

"You shouldn't have gone to the trouble," Arania said modestly as she opened the parcel. Suddenly she let out a shriek of delight. "Oh, Lysander, thank you, thank you! `Tis beautiful!" She held up the lovely red dress for her parents to see.

"`Tis a marvelous dress," Helene said happily. "Lysander, how did you ever afford such a thing?"

"We didn't buy it, Graciela`s mother made it herself." Lysander felt very proud indeed of his friend.

Arania stood up and hugged her brother tightly. "Tell her she has my most sincere thanks."

It was now time for Arania to go up to bed, and for Lysander to return to his own house so he could rest for work the next day. It was very cold as he walked home alone, but the snow and wind had stopped to reveal a clear black sky speckled with stars here and there.

Lysander had just enjoyed the best Christmas that he could remember, but Arania`s flushed and exhausted face kept swimming into his mind. He did not like it; he felt almost certain that she was beginning to fall ill again.

Lysander went back to his parents' house the next day, and made a fortifying elixir of Goldenrod and Camphor for Arania. At his insistence she went to bed a bit earlier than usual after putting in another full days work, and in a few days she was looking a bit better.

On the last night of December Lysander traded in his orderly uniform for his only suit and was at his parents' house by six thirty- the ball was to begin at seven.

"Arania will be down in a moment," his mother told him. She went back upstairs to tell Arania that Lysander had arrived, and within minutes his sister descended the wooden staircase from her room.

She was wearing the red silk dress and a pair of silver earrings borrowed from their mother. She smiled nervously at her brother, who returned it with love and pride.

"You look wonderful," he said with complete sincerity. Red really was the perfect color for her.

"Thank you."

"But something is missing." He reached into his pocket and pulled out a silk ribbon exactly the same shade of red as Arania's dress. Carefully he tied back his sister's long, gleaming hair and said, "Now you're ready."

Helene hugged Arania tightly. "Aye. Do enjoy yourselves, and be safe. Arania, dear, remember that you are to be home by nine this evening."

"Aye, Mama, I will." Arania took her brother's hand and the two walked out into the night.

"That Hyman Arevrel is one lucky lad," Lysander said as he helped Arania into the wagon. "You will be meeting him there?"

"Aye. And what about you? Are you not going with anyone?"

"Graciela has kindly consented to attend the dance with me. I must say, I never thought she had a liking for such affairs."

"`Twill be a pleasure to see her again," agreed Arania as they set off.

Fifteen minutes later they arrived at the palace, which was located in the very center of the city. Once there a sentry at the door found their name on the list of guests and admitted them into the entryway.

"Oh, `tis beautiful," Arania gasped. "Beautiful!" The high ceiling was adorned with golden cherubim, and festive wreaths hung on the walls. A crystal chandelier hung down, casting rainbow patterns of light onto the floor, and as she walked under it her eyes reflected a jewel-like sparkle.

They proceeded into the crowded dance hall, decked out in pale gold, and Dr. Barkoli approached them.

"Welcome, Lysander, welcome," he said happily. "So pleased that you could come. And Miss Arania, how lovely you look this evening." He grasped her hand, and she flushed pink, but returned his smile.

"Thank you."

"Thank you, Sir."

"Do come in," said the elderly physician amicably, and he gestured into the large room.

The two siblings entered, and were hailed by many of Lysander's coworkers.

Finally, as they passed the long table at the back laden with refreshments, Arania cried out, "Look, there's Graciela." and the young woman glided over to them, radiant in a dress of emerald green satin.

"Lysander!" she cried out jubilantly. "Arania. I was wondering where you had gotten to. `Tis so good to see you again."

"Good evening." Lysander beamed at his friend.

"Hello," Arania said happily, pleased to see the kind young woman. "I hope you have had a pleasant holiday?"

"Aye, `twas very fine. I saw you sing in the choir on Christmas day, Arania. You are a very talented girl."

"Thank you." Arania beamed. She looked over to the end of the ballroom and saw her own date at the doorway. "I must be off, Hyman is waiting for me."

She walked over to him, leaving the two young coworkers alone.

"Would you care to dance, Miss Graciela?" Lysander asked playfully.

"I would love to," Graciela laughed, and they began waltzing around the room to a fast-paced lindy.

"Arania has become a beautiful young lady, don't you agree?" asked Graciela, who was watching Lysander's sister as she danced with Hyman.

"Aye. We can't thank you enough for that heavenly gown, `twas her favorite gift by far. She was nervous about meeting Dr. Barkoli in a social atmosphere, but she seems to be enjoying herself. Who would have guessed four years ago that she would be dancing like she is now?"

"I know what you mean. I used to wonder if this career would suit me, being generally a man's occupation. It came as quite a surprise to me how much I loved it."

"Aye?" Lysander inquired surprised. "I never knew you thought that."

"Well, it was either that or be a scullery maid for the rest of my days." She snorted. "I hardly think anything could be worse than being someone's servant."

"Yes, I suppose you might argue that." Lysander grinned. "You really are perfectly suited to it, you know. By the way, is Dr. Barkoli going to have you working on a different set of hours? He sent me a telegram saying he wishes for me to start working in the hospital over the New Year."

"Nay, he has me doing exactly the same hours, but I am to be transferring to the East wing. Dreadful epidemic of Typhoid, as I am sure you know, people are dropping left and right." She shook her head in disgust. "Such a waste, and so soon after the war, too."

"Aye. Well, I've no doubt that he made the right decision."

She beamed at him, her smile more radiant than he could ever remember. "Thank you, Lysander! Did he tell you what wing you are to be stationed at?"

"The North wing. I just hope that Arania doesn't fall ill: it would be my doing."

"Lysander, don't be so foolish," admonished Graciela. "Nothing bad will happen to Arania with you around that is perfectly clear to me."

"You do know how to reassure us fools," he said, beaming at her.

"What are Arania's plans for future?" Graciela asked, watching the younger girl again. "She is nearly of the proper age to begin going to the university. Does she intend to go?"

"I don't know. Sometimes I think she would be an obvious choice to be accepted there-she is very bright. But she does so love working alongside our parents. She might think it impertinent of me to suggest that she leave them behind to pursue her own interests. I must say, though, that I have no doubt she would do the city a power of good."

"What field would she elect to go into if she did attend the university, do you think?"

"Well…" Lysander regarded his sister thoughtfully. "I always thought she would be a good healer. She already knows the uses of half the herbs we have been introduced to, and how to prepare and combine them. And she is so kind!" He sighed. "I just hope she can find her greatest joy and feel free to go after it, whatever it might be. I don't want her to suffer the stigma I did."

"Aye." Graciela's green eyes looked troubled, as though she did not trust herself to speak, before finally saying, "Things are better for you now, though, are they not?"

"Somewhat better. I think Papa is beginning to understand how much it means to me to be working in the hospital. There is no higher compliment than being trusted with another's welfare."

"Yes, I conquer."

Just then a much slower song, beautiful and mournful at the same time, began to swell throughout the room. Every couple began to dance slowly and gracefully, twirling across the floor in time to the crystalline trill of the flutes and honey-gold timbre of the guitars.

"Oh, I love this song!" Graciela exclaimed, and she began to hum along to the music, her eyes closed in a transport of happiness. "'Tis so beautiful."

"Aye. But not as beautiful as you, Miss Graciela," He grinned, pleased that she seemed to be so enjoying herself. "I wasn't sure if you would come tonight at all. I know how you dislike frivolities and such."

"I am an employee of the best physician in Bucharest," she returned, "And I will do what is expected of me as such." However, her words held no real heat, and her expression remained placid. That was one good thing about Graciela: she was not easily offended. "Besides," she added, opening her eyes again and looking directly into his, "The Company is infinitely better than the last time I came here."

"You've come here before?" Lysander could not believe his ears.

"Aye. Only once, quite some time ago. It was for a Christmas celebration, much like tonight. I was scarcely older than Arania is, and very bored. There were not many other children there, I did not feel like dancing because of the lateness of the hour, and I was wishing fervently that I were back home. My father was an employee of the host, you see, old Mr. Phietman, from the bank, before he died." Here she frowned. "Horrible old spendthrift, you know." Her eyes were so narrow that they were slits now: a long moment elapsed in silence as the pair of them continued to dance.

"He had a nephew," Graciela suddenly resumed, continuing to frown, and she shook her head. "I met him a few years previously when my father started working for the bank, we ended up going to the same grammar school. And he was a pest if I ever knew one. He used to think it was funny to put grass snakes in girls` shoes when they would play hopscotch, and he set beetles on them in the classroom. But that night at the Christmas ball, he outdid himself, he did."

"It started at around midnight. He approached me, looking very solemn, and asked if I would spare a dance for him. Being the daughter of an employee, I could not, of course, refuse. So I agreed, and he took my hand and led me out to the dance floor."

Here she shuddered, then resumed her story. "His hands were rough as a cats tongue, completely red and raw. And there was a glint in his eyes that I had seen all too often before: he looked as malevolent as ever with that sneer on his face. Still, I did not believe he would dare try anything ridiculous in front of his father, let alone a hundred or more respectable guests. He danced with me through a number of different songs, though I wanted to shake him off more with each passing second, and then he did something very odd indeed."

"He led me to the very center of the dance floor, and then walked a short distance away, saying that he wanted to admire me in the light of the candles. The malevolent look in his eye became more and more pronounced: his sneer was growing into a wicked-looking smile, and it seemed incredible to me that the other guests did not notice it. I was about to call out to him, to ask him exactly what he thought he was doing, but the question died on my lips that very second."

Now Graciela sighed. "No sooner had my eyes locked onto his than a deafening roar filled the air, and I was thrown backwards off my feet, landing hard on a chair several feet away. He had planted firecrackers underneath the platform where the band stood: they were all severely injured by the blast. I myself found that my ankle was sprained too badly to walk, and I had a bleeding gash on my forehead from hitting the chair with such an impact."

"Well, as you can imagine, that put a very abrupt end to the celebration. My father took me to the hospital, and the doctor said I was lucky to have escaped alive. The wound on my forehead required stitches, and I had to remain in the hospital for a fortnight until my ankle mended. Thankfully I never saw the little pest again: he was sent to a boarding school on the other side of the country." As Graciela spoke, she put a hand to her forehead, and Lysander noticed, for the first time ever, a two-inch long scar at the place where her fingertips rested, just above her right eye.

"Well," he supplied, "I don't doubt that he would not dream of doing such a horrible thing now, wherever he might be. A gentleman who mistreats a lady is no gentleman at all."

"Oh, I can laugh about it now," she said. "All things heal with time: people and feelings and relationships, too." She looked over at Hyman. "So, this Hyman Arevrel. Do you know much about him?"

Lysander followed her gaze. "Well, I heard that he is one of the best students, and is never disrespectful. I should have guessed as much. Arania would never hold with behavior like that."

"Knows how to choose them, does she?" Graciela smiled. "He seems pleasant enough."

"We aren't all charlatans," Lysander teased her.

The pair continued to dance, and before long the enormous Grandfather clock in the corner of the room was chiming nine `o clock.

"Drat, it's nine already," muttered Lysander. "Graciela, I must be off. I promised Mama and Papa that I would have Arania home by now, they are going to be furious with me."

"Until we meet again," was her reply, and she curtseyed to him. "I will see you at the hospital tomorrow, will I not?"

"Aye." He returned her curtsey with a steady, poised bow. "Good night, Miss Vendilan."

"Good night, Master Hiestad." She beamed at him as he walked off. He did not like leaving so suddenly, but he was certain that she would have no trouble in finding a new dance partner: she was very good looking, after all.

Arania bade her own date good night, and the two siblings exited the palace and climbed once more into their wagon.

A strong, bitter wind had picked up over the duration of the ball, and the ride back home was silent. Lysander felt so cold he was sure his hands were freezing to the reins as he conducted the horses forward.

Arania sat very still, only putting a hand to her mouth to stifle a periodic bout of coughing. Her eyes were almost completely closed, and, glancing at her out of the corner of his eye, he noticed that she was very pale.

The ride home seemed to take much longer than the ride into town, but finally the siblings arrived back at home. Lysander helped his sister down from the wagon and they quickly hurried inside.

"Ah, my dears, you are home!" cried Helene, hurrying to them when they entered the house. "I was most alarmed when this dreadful storm blew up, I was about to send a telegram to the constable." She helped Arania to take off her coat and the three of them sat before the fire. "Did you quite enjoy the ball?"

But Lysander never got the chance to reply, for at that moment mother and son were distracted by Arania, who began to cough terribly, unable to stop herself for many moments. She sank to her knees on the floor, gasping for breath.

"Arania," said Lysander, alarmed, putting his hands on her shoulders. "Are you all right?"

She did not respond immediately: her face had gone very white and she was breathing haggardly.

"Aye," she finally said in a weak voice. "I-I'm fine."

He put a hand to her forehead. "Hmm, you do feel quite warm." He helped her to her feet. "Come, it's high time you were in bed."

Helene helped Arania into her nightgown, and when she was in bed Lysander put a cool rag to her forehead to control her temperature. "We'll send for Dr. Barkoli in the morning," he said. "He'll have you feeling better in no time; I don't think it's anything more than a slight fever."

"Aye. Thank you, Lysander." Arania laid back on the pillow and was soon asleep.

He went to the door, pausing only once to look back at his sister, then left the room.

The wind was as fierce as ever when he walked along the high street back towards his own house: his lantern barely illuminated the darkness ahead of him.

However, his thoughts were far from the inclement weather.

He looked up into the stormy sky. A few little stars were visible here and there through the clouds of snow being blown all around him.

Finding a particularly bright one, he closed his eyes for a brief moment and said an unspoken prayer.

Dear Lord, he thought fervently. *Please protect my little sister. She is so good and brave, and I could not imagine life without her.*

He had done all he could for one night, he told himself as he opened his front door. No point in fretting over what he could not help.

The following morning, Arania fell to the floor the moment she tried to get up out of bed. The sound brought her mother running up to her room.

"Arania! What has happened to you?" She knelt beside her daughter.

"I'm okay, Mama," Arania said weakly. "I'm just a bit tired, I didn't sleep well last night." She tried again to stand, but fell to her knees. Her face was pale, and she was breathing heavily and perspiring.

Helene put a hand to her forehead. "Good Heavens, you are burning with fever! Get you back into bed at once." She helped her daughter back into bed, and hurried to make a telegram.

Meanwhile at the hospital Dr. Barkoli and his assistants were particularly busy. So naturally, when he received the telegram, he was less than pleased.

"Lysander, I must go to make a house call. Please brew a new batch of Camphor and Jasmine, there is a young boy who has recently undergone an amputation and is in need of careful monitoring."

"Aye, sir," Lysander said, and he headed back to the infirmary.

It was going to be a very long day.

After a thirty minute drive the elderly physician pulled up to the address stamped upon the telegram: a small cottage that bore all the visages of a hard-wrought, meager livelihood. He knocked on the door and within a few moments it was opened by a familiar, thin face above a worn homespun dress. Helene Heistad, Lysander's mother. Her yellow hair was frizzy and streaked with considerably more gray than the last time he had seen her, and her face wore a very frightened look indeed.

"Good Morrow, Madame," he said, as she beckoned him inside. "What seems to be the trouble?"

"My little daughter, Arania, has taken very ill," said Helene Heistad, in a constricted voice. Her gray-blue eyes were shining with unshed tears.

"Where is the poor child?"

"Upstairs." Helene led the way up the creaky wooden staircase and into Arania's room, where the girl lay under her blankets, coughing. After several moments she was still, though her eyes were unfocused.

"Arania," the physician said softly, "It's Dr. Barkoli. Can you hear me?"

Her eyes found him as he approached. "Aye," she said weakly.

Dr. Barkoli knelt beside the bed and felt the glands in her neck, which were very swollen. He listened carefully to her heart rate before repositioning the stethoscope with a frown. Then he found the pulse in her wrist and monitored it several moments, still frowning.

"She must be bled," he said finally. "The disease needs to be purged from her blood before she will recover." He opened his medical bag and took out a small basin and a case of lancets, from which he chose the smallest and sharpest of the lot.

Helene grasped her daughter's hand as the physician pushed up the sleeve of her nightgown. "Keep still, Arania," he instructed, and he made a small cut in the girl's arm. Bright red blood trickled steadily from the wound, and he held the basin up to the cut. "There we are." When the basin was filled he bandaged the wound and pulled the sleeve back down.

Next Dr. Barkoli produced a pouch of Lemongrass and Thyme, and emptied the contents into a kettle of water over the fire, keeping watch over the mixture as it boiled.

"Pneumonia," he said finally. "A stubborn case, it is true, but very treatable with a fever-reducing draught and plenty of rest. Arania will need to be closely monitored for the first few days, but I am confident that she will recuperate in due course."

When the medicine was ready, the physician poured it into a glass: it was pale green and thick as mud. "Now then, my dear," he said to Arania, "I have some medicine for you." He helped her to sit up and raised the glass to her mouth. The concoction was bitter as gall, but she drank it down without any bother. "That's a good girl," he said kindly.

Finally, when the girl could take no more of the medicine, he laid her back down, and her eyes promptly closed.

Turning back to Arania's mother, he handed her a larger pouch of the herbs. "Here. Give her a dose of this every three hours, and keep the fire in the hearth going: she must be kept warm. Don't hesitate to contact me if you require any assistance."

"Very well." Helene looked over at the slumbering child. "You have my deepest gratitude."

While they waited for their employer to return, Lysander and Graciela took it in turns to keep watch over the potion as it brewed and to tend to the boy, making sure he was kept clean and comfortable.

"Here, this will help with the pain," Graciela said to him, handing him a small cup of potion. She checked his temperature. "You feel a bit warm, are you well?"

"Aye," he said. "Just a bit sore."

She changed the bandage over the wound. "You seem to be healing well. Try to get some sleep, I'll return to check up on you later."

The boy leaned back on his pillow and was soon asleep. Graciela pulled a blanket up over him. "Rest peacefully," she said gently as she left the room.

Walking back to the waiting room, she found Lysander updating the registry.

"How is the lad?" he asked, looking up from the books.

"He is well. Sleeping at the moment. I do hope he recovers soon." Graciela was not usually one to fret, but her face was lined with concern. Seeing Lysander looking at her with concern, she cleared her throat abruptly and asked, "Has Dr. Barkoli not returned yet?"

"Nay," Lysander replied. He looked at the grandfather clock in the hallway. "It's been nearly two hours. Whomever he has gone to see must be frightfully ill."

Just then the aged physician entered. "There are five other physicians in this town," he said unhappily. "Why could they not enlist another? She would receive better care from a hospital not so overrun."

"You are the best, sir, everyone knows it," Lysander said. "The girl is in need of the best physician. I've no doubt you'll set her right yet."

As Lysander walked home that evening he could not help but think of how exhausted his sister had looked after the ball. Was it possible that the desperately ill girl was Arania? *Perhaps I should go home and check on her,* he thought fretfully.

But he had seen his sister for himself, had he not? There was nothing Dr. Barkoli would not easily be able to put to rights. He trusted his employer, and so did his family.

The following day everything went wrong at the clinic. Lysander was late to work, he accidentally burned a batch of Globe Mallow root and Fuganeek, which he was then made to gouge out of the cauldron, and he made mistake after mistake in the register, which took much time and effort to rectify. He was preoccupied, and everyone knew it. Somehow he knew he should have gone home the night before.

Finally, at around noon, a distraction was provided to take Lysander out of his tortured thoughts when a little girl, no older than six or seven, was rushed into the hospital.

"What seems to be the trouble?" Dr. Barkoli asked, carefully laying the child down on an exam table.

"She fainted this morning," said the child's mother fearfully. "I thought she was done for."

Dr. Barkoli examined the child, taking her pulse and listening to her breathing. He listened to her heartbeat, then replaced the stethoscope, frowning.

"We will have to bleed her," he said grimly. "Madame, if you would kindly step out for a moment- this is not something you ought to see."

"No!" shrieked the mother. "Don't, I beg of you, don't cut her!"

"It must be done," said the physician firmly. "She will surely perish if the Pestilence is not drained from her system. We will not injure her, I promise you."

Sobbing, the terrified mother permitted an orderly to lead her back out into the waiting area.

Dr. Barkoli produced a miniscule lancet from his medical bag. "Lysander, hold her tightly," he instructed. "It is crucial that she not move. I don't want to have to do this twice."

Lysander stood at the head of the exam table and held the little girl still, keeping a gentle but firm grip on her shoulders as his employer made a small incision in her right arm and filled two five-milliliter pans. She gasped in pain, but did not scream as he had feared she might.

"Don't look, dear," he said gently, brushing her bangs off of her burning forehead. "Keep your eyes on me. It will be over in a moment, just stay still. I know it hurts."

She looked up at him and some of the pain she was valiantly trying to hold in seemed to leave her face when she saw his warm smile.

"That's it. You're doing great."

Finally Dr. Barkoli bandaged the wound. "There we are little one." To his employee he said, "Someone will have to stay with her while I prepare an elixir to fight the infection. Take her to recovery, Lysander, make sure she is comfortable, I will be back shortly."

"Am-am I dying?"she asked in a weak voice.

"Nay, little one," Lysander said. "We won`t let that happen." It would be a struggle to save her, he knew, but it was a struggle he would endure gladly.

"I was so scared when Dr. Barkoli said he would have to bleed me," the child-her name was Julinne-informed him. "Thank you for calming me."

"It was a pleasure." Lysander smiled at his little patient, glad that this, at least, had gone right for him today. "You were very brave."

Suddenly she looked past him, to the door, trying to sit up. "Where is my mother? She must be frantic."

"She`s filling out registration forms in the lobby," he answered, continuing to mop her brow. "Don`t talk now, sweetheart, you need to rest."

"But I...." she began, and then she lapsed into a fit of coughing.He knew she should not be so worked up when she was this ill; her small body was nearly overwhelmed by the fever as it was.

"Shh. We`re going to get you healed, don`t fear." Lysander took both her hands in his and massaged them gently, and slowly the fretful expression left her face. "That`s it." He smiled at her. "Good girl. Dr. Barkoli will be back in a moment with some medicine for you, just hold on."

Julinne smiled a sweet, shy smile back at him. The cold compress seemed to be doing her some good; her face was less flushed than before.

At that moment a loud shouting could be heard from the waiting area, and Dr. Barkoli entered the exam room, looking completely exasperated.

"Lysander, your father is out front. He wishes to speak with you."

"I can't leave," Lysander said, hating how stubborn he sounded. "There is no one else to stay with this child. She needs to be looked after."

"You must, he is in a red rage. Graciela will take over for you. Go now, quickly."

Lysander sighed. He did not want to face his father today, not when he was already exhausted. But he knew it would be the worse for him if he delayed.

"I have to go, Julinne," he told the little girl. "I'll be back in a moment." And he walked out into the waiting room.

The moment he saw his father's livid expression Lysander knew he would not be returning to work that day. Regalus glared at him and bellowed, "Boy! Get you home! You shall not waste time on strangers when your own sister needs you."

Biting back the angry retort on his tongue, Lysander asked, "What's happened? I thought she was just worn out. I don't understand."

"Nor do I," said his father grimly, "But I can tell you that the poor girl has never been so ill. Barkoli was wrong. I-" and here he faltered, his brown eyes wide, "I fear she may be near the end."

"Take me to her," Lysander said grimly.

Father and son trudged home through a snowy storm for what seemed like hours, the latter cursing himself with every step. *I knew there was something wrong with her that night after the ball,* he fumed inwardly. *I should have gone to her. How could I have been so stupid?*

Finally they reached the house, and Lysander ran inside.

"Arania! Arania!" He pelted up the staircase and into his sister's bedroom.

It was hot in the small room, a blazing fire roared in the fireplace. Their mother had been sitting by

Arania`s side, putting a damp rag to her brow. When her husband and son entered the room, she stood and walked over to them, terror in her face. "Regalus, I've no idea what to do. Barkoli`s prescriptions have been no help for her."

Lysander took his mother's place at Arania`s side. He took her pulse, racing beneath her veins. He put the back of his hand to her forehead; she felt hot as fire.

"She has Typhoid," he finally said, with as much composure as he could muster while his heart filled with terror.

"Good Lord, why take that poor child?" Helene groaned. She sounded faint. Typhoid was a dreaded disease, nearly always fatal.

"`Twill not take my sister," Lysander said firmly. "I'll not allow it. Mama, put a kettle on to boil, I must make an elixir to fight the infection."

Helene left the room, and reappeared almost at once with a kettle of water, which she put on the trivet over the fire. Meanwhile Lysander prepared a mixture of wild Mint, Fuganeek and Goldenrod, all the while keeping his eyes on his sister. How painful it was to see her like this, so ill that she could not keep her eyes open!

The water was boiling now; he added the herbs and let them simmer while he picked up the rag and mopped Arania's feverish brow, feeling horrible guilt.

After a minute or two her eyes opened halfway. "Who's there?" she asked very weakly. "Lysander?"

"Be still, sister," he said gently. "I'm right here. I'll take care of you."

She grinned weakly at him. "I never doubted that you would."

He grinned back. Such a sweet child!

He poured the drought into a glass. "Here, drink this." He carefully lifted his sister's head up and fed the medicine to her slowly so she wouldn't choke. "There we go. That's a good girl."

When she had taken as much of the medicine as she could, he laid her carefully back down and pulled the blanket up around her. Immediately her eyes fluttered closed.

"Will she recover?" Helene asked tentatively.

"No one is more deserving of God's mercy than Arania," Lysander said firmly. "He will not take her from us." He looked at his mother. "Get you some sleep, Mama. I'll stay with her."

Meanwhile, back at the hospital, Graciela Vendillan had resumed Lysander's vigil at Julinne's side, monitoring her vital signs as she waited for Dr. Barkoli to return with the elixir needed to fight the fever-if only that could be lowered, she would recuperate.

She looked over at the clock in the lobby and scowled. Why Lysander had chosen now to run off, she had no idea, but it was very unlike him to behave in such a way with a desperately ill child to look after. She only hoped it was important.

She was recalled to her present when Julinne let out a low groan of pain. Placing a cool hand to the little girl's forehead, she whispered, "Shh. Don't move, it's all right. I'm right here." The child went still at her touch, and her eyes opened.

"Who-are you?"

"I'm Nurse Vendillan," Graciela said softly to her. "I'm going to take care of you, Julinne."

"Where is Dr. Heistad?"

The young nurse sighed. "I don't know, sweetheart."

Julinne frowned. "I miss him."

Graciela smiled. "He is very kind, isn't he? Don't worry, I'm sure he will be back soon."

At that moment Dr. Barkoli entered the room. "How is she holding up?"

"Not well," said Graciela grimly. "The fever keeps climbing, she can't fight it much longer."

The elderly physician approached their tiny patient. "Julinne? It's Dr. Barkoli. Can you hear me, dear?"

"Aye," the child groaned, her eyes unfocused. "Everything is so dizzy."

"Here, this will help." He raised her head up, and lifted the wooden cup of elixir to her mouth. She began to drink, but then stopped as she lapsed into a fit of coughing, and then she began to vomit a poisonous-looking black bile all over the bedspread.

"Graciela, help me with her," the physician commanded, and together they held Julinne up in a sitting position. "Hold on, my child," he said to the girl as she wretched.

Julinne continued to vomit for many moments, until, gasping for breath, she stopped. Her eyes were wide in dismay as she looked down at the black mess that covered the topmost blanket. "I`m so sorry," she said miserably.

"It`s quite all right," Dr. Barkoli assured her as he wiped the residue from her lips with a clean rag, and Graciela removed the soiled blanket to the washroom. "We have to purge the pestilence from your system. You`re on the way to recuperating, Julinne." He laid her back down carefully and covered her with another warm blanket.

In a moment Graciela had returned with a wooden cup of water. She helped Julinne to drink some, then said, "Well, that was fast. Normally they don`t start purging the pestilence for twelve hours."

"She`s not out of the woods yet, I`m afraid," replied the physician. "She is still very ill. We will need to bleed her again in a day or two."

Julinne looked up at them, her eyes wide with terror.

"Don`t be afraid," Graciela said to her, and she grasped the little girl`s icy-cold hand. "I`ll be right there, I promise."

"We won`t hurt you, child," Dr. Barkoli said. "You are in good hands."

Julinne smiled, though it cost her every ounce of strength she possessed. "Thank you." And within the space of a few moments, she had fallen soundly asleep.

Dr. Barkoli sighed. "What a disgrace it is when a child faces down death," he muttered. He went to the door. "Let`s let her rest for awhile."

Out in the hallway, Graciela looked at her employer. "So where is Lysander, anyway?"

The elderly physician sighed, and suddenly looked much older. "He had to go home. His sister is ill."

"Arania….no," Graciela gasped. "No, not her."

"Aye." Dr,. Barkoli looked worried. "I made a house call a few days ago, and I thought I could salvage her. She must have taken a turn for the worse, what with this horrid cold. I will have to go and see if there is not more I can do for her."

"But that would be impossible," Graciela said. "We cannot manage without you; we need every available pair of hands to help out here. Lysander has been trained well," she added, as much to herself as to her employer, "He will be able to cure Arania, I know it."

Over the next two days Lysander tended to his sister whenever he was not at work. He tried everything he knew, but Arania did not recuperate. In fact, she appeared to be getting worse. Her skin was pale as clean ice, her small body shook with coughs, and she shivered night and day in a horrid chill, although they kept the fire on the hearth roaring.

"Lysander," she said weakly, on the third night, as her brother took her pulse. "I have one last favor to ask of you, for I will be gone by morning, and there is no one whom I trust more."

"Don't say such things," Lysander admonished, and there was a definite note of anguish in his voice. "I'll cure you, I promise. You're going to be fine." But he knew deep down that the odds were almost completely against him.

Arania placed her small hand inside his. "Don't torment yourself, dear brother. You cannot cure me, no one can." She looked at him calmly, and he felt wonder in her strength of spirit. "Oh Lysander, I love you with all my soul."

"And I you, my precious little sister." Lysander was fighting back tears now: he did not want to let them fall in front of Arania.

"You are an incredible healer," she continued, keeping those calm eyes on him. "I have never known anyone so kind. My one wish is to have the certainty that you will always be as compassionate as you are now. I want to be assured that you will always care for those who need you, wherever you go."

"That is a promise." He leaned over and kissed her cheek gently, not sure how much longer his resolve would hold.

Arania`s eyes suddenly widened, and he realized that she was looking at something behind them. "Lysander, look. Look at the night sky. Have you ever seen anything so beautiful?"

Lysander looked out the window and saw that she was right. Thousands of stars were glittering like diamonds against the black sky, and the moon loomed above them like an enormous gold coin.

"Aye," he finally agreed. "`Tis an arresting sight indeed."

Just then she started coughing, and he pulled the blanket higher up over her.

"Easy. Easy, Arania." He stroked her tangled hair in a soothing manner, and she was still, her eyes closed. "There we go. Rest peacefully, sweetheart."

For a few minutes he simply sat there and watched her small chest rise and fall, thanking God that she was alive.

She's just frightened, he thought, willing himself to believe it. *I'll heal her. It's not over.*

He was exhausted himself, and within a few minutes he also had fallen asleep in the chair where he sat.

The next morning Lysander was awakened by strong sunshine coming through the window. He looked outside: it was a beautiful winter day.

"Arania, it's morning," he said, turning to his sister.

She did not move. "Arania? Arania, wake up." He shook her shoulder.

"Arania, no! No!"

But he knew she could not hear him. She was gone, just as she had predicted. With a groan of despair, he dropped his head onto the blankets, his hand less than an inch from hers.

Arania`s funeral took place two days later, and Lysander could not remember a more desperately sad occasion. His mother sobbed without restraint. Lysander's eyes, however, remained dry. His grief was beyond tears.

He kept his eyes on Arania while the priest said a sermon over her still body, not taking in a word of it. They had decided to bury her in her best holiday dress, and he could not remember when she had looked so beautiful. Had it really been only a week ago that she had been dancing at the Yule ball, lively and joyful? He did not even notice the cold.

The next few days passed in a haze of pain and disbelief for the family. Slowly, Regalus and Helene began functioning again, disheartened though they were. Lysander, however, remained completely disconsolate. His grief for his beloved little sister had consumed him.

One night a week after Arania had died, Helene peered out the window to see her son alone in the courtyard of the small church across the road. He knelt at one of the grave markers, cold moonlight washing over him. She did not need to see the inscription upon the granite to know that it was her daughter's grave at which he knelt.

She put on her coat and walked out and across the road towards him. "Lysander! LYSANDER!" She called his name as she entered the wrought iron gate surrounding the courtyard, but he did not move from where he knelt.

Finally she reached him. Dressed in a dark coat and black gloves, he looked quite forbidding with his face set in a scowl as he stared stonily at the grave marker, daring passerby to disturb him.

Still, Helene knew he must be persuaded to leave this dreadful place. "Lysander, my love, come you into the house. `Tis too cold to be out here."

"`Tis colder for my little sister," said the youth bitterly. "And lonelier, to boot."

"You've no reason to feel ashamed. You tried your hardest, and we could not have asked more of you than that." Tears trickled down Helene's face. "You stayed with her the whole time. You comforted her."

"I was weak," he said angrily. "I fell asleep when I should have been watching over her. That was when it happened. I let her slip away." With a sigh of disgust, he put a hand upon the stone that bore his sister's name.

"You were exhausted; you had every right to a bit of sleep."

"Not when she was so ill. Not when I promised her that I would save her."

"Son," Helene began, and then she choked on her words and had to begin again. "You could not have saved her. That much was obvious to me when Barkoli's medicines failed to help. It was just her time."

At these words Lysander stood abruptly and turned on his mother. He was rather taller than she, and his face was etched with a fury she had never seen before. He looked absolutely bestial.

"Her time!" he shouted, his voice exploding through the silent darkness around them. *"Her time?! She was fourteen years old! A child! She never had a chance to live! And now she never will! Because of me! She's gone forever, and it's my fault!"* Angry tears sprang into his eyes, and he repeated, in a desolate whisper, "It's all my fault."

"Lysander, please, come you inside," Helene pleaded. Tears were pouring down her face now. "I cannot lose you too."

Lysander turned away from her, taking deep, shaky breaths to master himself. The clean, icy air was oddly welcome: it seemed to burn away some of his anger.

"I think I need to be alone, Mama," he finally said, relieved to hear his voice come out calm and controlled, "I just need to clear my head. I'll be back in a bit, don't wait up."

And with that he walked out of the courtyard and onto the road, leaving his sobbing mother beside the grave.

I'm sorry, he thought, not looking back. *I never meant to hurt you. I can only hope you'll forgive me someday. But I can't come back, not ever.*

He walked along the high street into town and eventually came to the hospital. Looking in through the window he saw little Julinne, lying fast asleep in the darkness. He had nearly forgotten her in the tragedy of losing his sister.... she had been so ill.... Guilt consumed him, and he thought,

She's not going to survive. She's not strong enough. She will die, because she needed me and I neglected her, as I did my sister. Dear Lord, why take her? It is one thing to punish me, but she wronged no one.

Suddenly, only dimly aware that he was doing so, he walked to the doors and let himself inside. Looking around the corridor, he saw to his relief that he was alone. He did not want to be seen. He quickly entered Julinne's room, the first to the left, and shutting the door silently behind him, he approached her. Up close, he saw that she was shivering in her slumber. Poor child.

Lysander tucked a second blanket around her tiny frame. "There we go, little

one." Immediately she fell still and sighed with relief. He brushed the bangs off of her forehead, noticing as he did so that she no longer burned with the horrid fever that had threatened her the week before. She *would* survive. And little though he felt like it, he smiled as he stroked her hair-after all, it was not the child's fault that she lived when his sister was gone.

"It's good to see you again," he whispered.

At that moment Julinne's eyes fluttered open. "Dr. Heistad?"

He smiled at her. "Hello, little one. How are you?"

"Better," she said, propping herself up on her elbows. "The fever has gone. Dr. Barkoli says I can go home in a few days."

"I am glad to hear it. I worried for you, you were very sick." He sat beside her. "Has your mother been to see you?"

"Every day. She's very grateful that you calmed me when Dr. Barkoli bled me." As she said this, he looked down and saw that her arms bore new lacerations; she had been bled twice more in his absence. He regretted not being there for that. Well, now was an opportune time to apologize.

"Listen, Julinne-I'm very sorry for leaving like that. It was an emergency. Someone else needed me."

'I know," said Julinne, and there was nothing accusatory in her voice at all. "I don't blame you. I hope they are all right?"

He smiled, just slightly, but she was too young to see the pain behind it. If she only knew!

"You are a sweet girl."

"Well, I am glad you have returned," she said drowsily, and she leaned back against the pillow. "We need you."

"You're going to be okay, Julinne," he said softly, grasping her hand as her eyes began to to close. "The good Lord will preserve you. Have a peaceful sleep, my dear."

At that moment a familiar voice said, "Lysander? What are you doing here?" He turned around quickly. Graciela stood in the doorway. "I thought you would be home caring for Arania."

"So you've heard about what happened to her," he said, looking at the floor.

"Aye. Dr. Barkoli told me." She approached very slowly, her expression pensive, as though she desired nothing more than to flee from his presence. "He said I would have to look after Julinne. But what are you doing here now? Visiting hours end at seven, you know that."

"I just wanted to see her one last time," he said simply. "I wanted to see that she was mending and to apologize for leaving."

"What do you mean, one last time?" Graciela demanded. "You're coming back to work once Arania has mended, aren't you?"

Lysander sighed miserably. He was determinedly looking anywhere but at Graciela, who was one of the strongest people he knew: He did not want to see her reaction to his terrible news.

"Graciela," he finally said, slowly, each word like a dagger to his heart, "she didn't mend. I tried everything I know. She's gone."

Graciela's brilliant eyes were clouded with misery, but she did not shed a tear. As in his case, her grief seemed too great to be expressed by merely crying.

"I am very, very sorry for you," she said at last, her voice thick with pain. "She was a wonderful child."

"Aye. Graciela, I have a favor to ask of you. Take care of Julinne. She needs you. Make sure she gets well."

"Me? But aren't you returning?"

For the first time that night he met her gaze. "I can't. I can't stay in this town. I'm reminded of my sister everywhere I go, reminded that I couldn't save her." He balled his hand into a fist. "I work at the best hospital in the country, and I couldn't do a thing for her."

Graciela sighed. "Oh, Lysander." She reached out and grasped his hand. He did not shrug out of her grasp but returned the gentle pressure.

"Do this one thing for me. Please." His eyes locked on hers, and she could see the seriousness in their dark depths. "I cannot allow this child's mother to suffer the same fate I have."

Graciela said nothing for a long while. She merely looked at him, and wondered how fate could be so cruel to someone as kind and compassionate as he was. Finally, she spoke, very softly.

"Aye." That was all she said, for that was all she needed to say. She understood completely.

He smiled joylessly. "I can always depend on you."

"May you find peace," Graciela said, and they hugged.

"Tell Julinne that it's not her fault I left," he said as he went to the door. "I want her to know that I do care about her."

"Aye." Graciela smiled sadly at him, which caused him untold pain. "Be well, Lysander." He walked out into the corridor and out the main entrance to the hospital.

He continued walking. Up the street a few blocks was his father's shop, neglected since Arania had died. Cobs of corn, heads of lettuce, tomatoes and beets lay in their crates, unopened and forgotten. He felt even worse upon seeing this, and continued on his way.

He continued to walk, his mind spinning.

On the one hand, he knew he could hardly be more selfish than this. His parents needed him to help supplement their income; that had been the whole reason for his going to the university in the first place. Dr. Barkoli and his coworkers needed him to manage at the hospital. He ached with sorrow at the thought of abandoning his patients, the innocent human beings who needed his care. Especially sweet, trusting little Julinne. And what about Arania? She had looked up to him all her life, had always counted on him to do the right thing. It would destroy her to see him behaving so childishly. But on the other hand, he would always be haunted by her death.

Oh, what does it matter? He thought. *What chance do I have of curing anyone when I failed to save my own sister? I wish she hadn't trusted me so, I never deserved it.*

He looked around. He was deep in the woods, completely alone except for the evergreen trees that were covered with snow, which glittered in the moonlight like diamonds. He could not enjoy the scenery, though, not without Arania to be there with him. He kept walking, neither knowing nor caring much where he would end up.

He had gone about half a mile when he suddenly stopped and listened. Was someone following him? He was sure he had heard footsteps behind him. He did not want to be seen, not tonight.

He listened harder. No doubt about it, there was someone following him.

Lysander picked up the pace, suddenly feeling very nervous. Who was it? What did they want?

"Go away!" he cried out, trying to keep the panic out of his voice. "Leave me alone!"

At that moment a loud cackling could be heard from behind him. He ran faster and faster, flying over the ground.

"Go away! Go away! Go away!"

He leapt over exposed tree roots and rocks, fought his way past the branches that seemed to be reaching out to grab him, and eventually found himself at a wide river, almost completely frozen solid. He stopped dead in his tracks: how on earth was he supposed to get across this?

The cackling voice was coming closer. There was nothing else for it: he would have to jump.

Lysander braced himself, then jumped through the thick gray ice. The frigid water went up to his chest. The rocks at the bottom were worn so slick that he nearly lost his footing and his legs became tangled in weeds. Finally, coughing and gasping for breath, he pulled himself onto the opposite bank with the little strength that remained to him.

He sat at the riverbank for a few moments, panting, and then slowly rose to his feet, listening hard. He heard nothing now but the wind, and saw nothing but his own footsteps leading into the river.

It's gone now, he thought. *Whatever it was, it's gone.* He sighed with relief. He looked around for a safe place to spend the night.

Finally he spotted a cave in the side of a hill about twenty meters away. It would be drafty, but it would have to do. He began gathering pieces of firewood and taking them into the cave.

Within five minutes he had a fire inside the cave. He sat there trying to warm himself, wondering what had been following him. He had never heard anything like that voice, a sharp, horrible crackling like a bolt of lightning. He wondered if he ought to stay there another night, just to make quite sure that he was not being followed.

The warmth of the fire was making him drowsy, and he soon was nodding off, despite the wind that was howling outside...

Several hours later, he awoke to find himself in complete darkness. The fire had blown out. He got up to relight it, but found that the wood had been dampened by snowfall. Cursing under his breath, Lysander walked out into the snowy midnight to find more wood.

He had just located a scattering of broken branches when he heard the evil-sounding laughter, a full-throated roar of triumph. He froze where he was, trying to locate the direction from which the terrifying sound came, but it seemed to be coming from nowhere and everywhere all at once.

"Leave me alone!" he shouted at it, anger and fear thundering through him in equal measure. *"Leave me alone!"*

And with that he took off once more, leaving his findings forgotten where they lay, thundering away from the cave faster than he had ever ran in his life.

When he finally stopped to catch his breath, he leaned against a large rock in the forest floor and looked around.

He knew at once that he had run deep into the very heart of the woods, a place he had never been to. Here the trees were much taller, and seemed to be a great deal older than those he usually saw on his Gathering expeditions. A dried-up creek lay to his left, and to his right a scattering of more large rocks, each the size of a Wolfhound.

He listened hard. No sign of the evil laughter now, there was silence but for the rushing of a moderate gale. He waited for his racing heart to return to normal, and then began walking; looking for a place to stay-it was far too cold to attempt continuing his walk tonight.

He leapt over the dried up creek, kicking up snow, and proceeded towards a small stone chapel, long since neglected. He felt satisfied: this would provide much better protection from the elements than the cave had.

He spotted a demolished tree, struck down by lightning, a few yards away, and grabbed an armload of wood from the pile. He deposited it on the floor of the stone chapel, very pleased with his findings. Soon he would have a proper fire and perhaps get himself reasonably warm.

Suddenly a black shadow flew menacingly over the moon, obstructing the light, just as Lysander had returned for a second armload of wood. He walked quickly towards his shelter, but suddenly felt the most peculiar sensation.

It seemed as though all his muscles had frozen at once: he could not move an inch no matter how hard he tried. He heard the demonic laughter again, louder and madder than ever, and also noticed a large pair of bulging, glowing, ruby-red eyes that bored into his. They seemed to be sapping every once of strength he possessed: he struggled furiously to turn away, but he could not. He felt his eyes begin to close, his heart rate slowing more and more as he succumbed to the horrible eyes' power.

All of a sudden he gave a yell of pain that could no doubt be heard all the way into the town. A piercing, burning ache pulsed at this neck, a sharp stabbing that was growing stronger by the second. He tried to run, but his legs would not work properly: they were paralyzed with dread. Two very powerful hands were gripping him by the shoulders, holding on very tightly. Feeling weaker and weaker by the second, Lysander managed to force his eyes open, and saw the most terrifying thing he had ever seen.

He had caught sight of his attacker through the haze of pain and weakness. A ghostly white head was at his neck, the teeth still gnawing at his flesh as the pain reached a pitch like he had never experienced before. Suddenly the head rose up, and Lysander saw the most hideous face he could imagine. Red, bulging eyes, a flat, snakelike snout, and a mouth full of long, pointed gray teeth, stained with blood-his blood, he realized. The monster laughed, the same evil sound he had been hearing all night, and then it bit him again. Lysander roared in pain, but he could not escape. His eyes were growing so very heavy, he was losing so much blood, he could not fight it... he lost consciousness.....

He awoke sometime later to find himself in the entryway of a large mansion. He knew not where he was, perhaps hundreds of miles from the place where he had fallen.

He looked around carefully. The place was ornately furnished, but very dark and austere looking. A spasm of fear shot through him: where was that monster hiding?

He began walking through the house. He passed a Sitting room, a Drawing room, a Ballroom, and finally he came to an Armory.

The latter was stocked with all manner of weapons, everything from revolvers to machetes, to battle axes of every size. Should he arm himself? Would a weapon be of much help against a creature that could sneak up upon him and attack without warning, drain him of his strength before he could even know what was happening?

In the end he selected the longest of the swords, the one with the thickest blade. At least it was something.

I just want to get out of this place! He thought impatiently.

Sighing, he began to walk through the corridors. He had not gone far when a hard blow sent him sprawling into the wall. Breathing hard, he looked around him and there he saw the monster. It swooped down at him, screeching like a deranged bat, and he just barely managed to dive away in time. Barely was he on his feet again when the vampire came at him again. It slashed at him with thick claws on its hands, leaving a deep bloodless gash in the youth's face.

Lysander had by now forgotten his fear; he was filled instead with rage. Snarling in a beast-like way, he punched his attacker, sending him reeling to the floor. The vampire screeched again, louder this time, and threw Lysander with all his strength.

He hit the display case, and broken glass rained down upon him like knives. The swords that were displayed in the case were knocked off of their stands and landed beside him. Dazed, he shook his head to clear it, then leaped up and charged at his foe, brandishing his sword and shouting the types of words that would turn his mother's hair white.

The vampire, however, merely laughed, a dry, harsh laugh that more resembled a fit of coughing, and raised a hand up. Lysander was thrown upwards before he came within ten inches of his attacker, and hit the ceiling with bone-wrenching force, and then plummeted back to the floor.

Raised himself up to glare at the vampire, who walked calmly over to him and kicked him so that he crumpled back to the floor.

"Who are you?" he snarled, his gaze never wavering from the ghastly visage above him, feeling more furious than ever at the mocking smile on the pallid lips. "Where have you taken me? Why have you taken me from my home?"

The vampire laughed. Lysander had not known if he was capable of speech, but he said, in Lysander's own language, "This is your home now. Do not let thoughts of the past cloud your senses, boy." He had a dry, rough voice, like a crack of electricity.

"What are you talking about?! Tell me who you are!"

"I am the one nightmare you will never escape from, Lysander Heistad." Now a large yellow gemstone, set in a silver pendant around the vampire's neck, began to glow, first dully, then brighter and brighter.

"Behold. See what you have become." As Lysander watched, the pendant filled the entire room with a cold light. And in the light of the flashing stone, he saw a sight that was ten times more frightening than his assailant.

It was himself he saw reflected in the gemstones horrible, burning light-looking completely unlike himself. His eyes burned back at him with hatred, their warm brown turned to a glowing red. Horrible long fangs protruded from his mouth. Innumerable bloodless cuts and scrapes covered nearly every inch of his face. He hissed frightfully, furiously, and the terrible image of himself reflected in the bright light hissed also.

I'm just like him, he realized, feeling a pit of hopelessness open up inside him. *I'm a monster, just like he is.*

How he wished the creature had killed him that he was sleeping under the frozen ground, like his poor little sister! *Maybe I would be with her again if he had killed me*, he thought, breathless with grief.

The bright light grew stronger and stronger, searing Lysander's eyes, and he was forced to shut them. Heat filled the room, getting warmer and warmer until he was struggling to breathe.

He could not stay awake any longer, he collapsed on the floor.

"Get up." He felt a hard kick to the diaphragm, and grunted in pain. Panting, he rose to his feet, looking around.

He was surrounded by vampires. The one who had kicked him to consciousness laughed unpleasantly. He looked to be about the age of Lysander's father, with a battle-worn face and menacing black eyes that shone with malice, even in the dark.

"So, the new arrival. I can't say much for your taste in this one, Master."

"Probably never hunted a day in his life," said another, a young-looking man with brown hair and eyes like blue ice. "Didn't you say he ran instead of fighting? I have never heard of such a thing before."

"I value life," Lysander snarled. "I am a physician, a healer. Not a killer like you wretches."

"And a great physician you must be, too." This from a young woman to the right of the older of the two men. Lysander saw that she had flaming red hair and emerald-green eyes, exactly like Graciela, but her face had none of Graciela's gentle beauty. It was hard as stone, lined with dislike and disgust. "Abandoning that little girl in the hospital, caring naught if she lives or dies in your absence."

Lysander snarled at her. "She is *not* going to die!"

The older man snorted derisively.

"Oh yes, just like sweet little Arania. She perished while you slumbered beside her, without a care in the world, didn't she? You failed a defenseless child."

How did they know about Arania? About his stupidity, his cowardice, his failures? Lysander could feel himself losing control.

"Don't you speak of my sister, you arrogant bastard! Don't you dare!"

He grabbed the sword he had dropped and lunged at the vampire, but the latter was prepared for his assault. A bolt of lightning issued from his fingertips and shot Lysander in the chest, throwing him backward into the wall. The vampire laughed maniacally, and then shot Lysander with lightning once more.

"That is quite enough," said the familiar, cracking voice from behind him. Lysander whirled around and saw the white-faced, red-eyed vampire.

"I tell you again, Grovanich, we must expand our army of undead. We must not throw away any chance to increase our strength. Besides, time will change his attitude, I do not doubt." A frown formed on his ugly face.

"Master Morugan."

"Not another word, you fool! To the observatory with you, we must keep watch over the moon cycles."

Grovanich scowled. "Very well, my lord." And he departed, muttering furiously under his breath all the while.

"Ignatio, Padmona, be off with you. I wish to speak with our new friend alone."

The two youths exited, leaving Lysander alone with the Head Vampire, the dreadful Morugan. He breathed hard through his flat, snakelike snout, glaring at the youth.

"Now then, we will have no more trouble from you, or I shall take your life myself. Do not underestimate my might, or my conviction, for I have seen hell itself and triumphed." With that he threw Lysander to the side of the room, and then left, magiking the door shut behind him.

Lysander gave a bestial roar and launched himself at the door, pummeling it with his fists. "Let me out of here! *Let me out! You can't do this!*"

He shouted and raged and did his best to break down the door, but it was of no use. The Head Vampire's enchantment held the door shut tightly. Finally, after nearly an hour, all the fight had gone out of him.

He sank to the floor, exhausted, and pulled a small, paper-thin portrait of Arania from his pocket. It had been done just over a year ago, when she had moved on to secondary school: he himself had painted it.

He could still remember that early autumn day; hear Arania laughing as she positioned herself on the chair, her brilliant eyes wide with excitement for the start of the new school year.

And then his own voice: *Almost done, my lovely one. This is going to be the best portrait we've made yet.*

Because I have the fortune of knowing the best painter. Go on, Lysander, you know it's true!

Arania, stay still, I haven't gotten your eyes just yet. There we are.

Perfect. So, are you excited to be starting secondary school?

Aye. I'm very excited.

It seems like only yesterday you were still ambling around in those braces, and now look at you. You'll be going to the university yourself in no time at all. Won't that be fine?

Aye. I can only hope that whatever I choose to study, I can be adept at it as you were.

I don't doubt that you will be. I'm very proud of you.

Lysander opened his eyes and recalled himself to his current situation. Looking down, he saw that a runaway tear had splashed onto the portrait. He carefully rubbed it away: this little piece of paper was all he had to remember his sister by now.

"I'm sorry, Arania." He sighed. "I miss you so much."

He looked out the window and saw that the sun was rising. Immediately he felt as though all the life was being squeezed out of him: pain was swelling up inside his chest, he could not breathe, and he was surely going to die.

Gasping for breath, he staggered a few paces towards the window and pulled the blinds shut.

The darkness was an indescribable relief: he drew in a deep breath and let it out slowly. Eventually his head stopped spinning and he stood upright. It was time to start planning for his escape from this place.

The next evening Lysander cautiously reopened the shutters. It was completely dark outside. It would be difficult to sneak past Morugan and his followers, but he needed to find a way to destroy the crystal the Head Vampire wore around his neck. That, he was sure, was the way to stop the hellish creatures. He might not be able to return to his family, but he was not going to spend his life here, trapped with these monsters.

The moon was bright, illuminating the vast expanse of snowy land around the mansion. Lysander cursed under his breath: he had not been counting on that. Well, too late to back out now.

He put on his jacket and gloves. The door was sealed, impenetrable, but he might be able to break open the window...

He walked over to it and attempted to push up the windowpane. It did not budge. He tried again, and the pane slid up a quarter of an inch...then a half an inch...

Bit by bit the windowpane slowly opened large enough for him to climb out.

The moment his boots landed in the snow, he began to feel a rush of suspense. If he was caught, he would be killed. It was as simple as that.

No. It was not an option. He had failed to save his sister's life, but he would not break his promise to her.

He began to walk as soundlessly as possible, realizing as he did so that he could hear sounds he had never noticed before. The rustle of a barely-there breeze, the scrape of one snowflake against another, the shriek of a bat a hundred miles away. His senses must have been heightened when Morugan bit him. If he could hear these sounds, it was a sure bet that the Head Vampire could. Why had he not been found out?

Lysander crept around to the other end of the house and peered into the adjacent window. There, clearly visible, was the gemstone, nestled in a locked glass case.

Would the vampire enter the room? Lysander could hear the footsteps in the corridor beyond...

He strained his ears harder...No, the footsteps were retreating. Taking a deep breath, he pushed up on this windowpane.

It took just as long to open this window as the first due to a thick coating of ice that encased the panes. However, he strained with all his strength, and eventually succeeded in opening this window. He quickly crawled inside.

Lysander looked around the ornate bedchamber. He did not doubt that the key was well hidden, and his ears were straining harder than they ever had before, waiting for Morugan to return. He opened the nightstand drawer. No key. He looked over to the desk. No key on top, nor in any of the drawers. He opened the armoire, peeled back the blood red carpet, and looked into the traveling bag hidden beneath the desk. No key anywhere within the room. Should he search the other rooms? Did he dare venture out and risk detection?

The mansion was enormous: searching thoroughly would no doubt take hours and he did not have hours to spare.

He jiggled the blade inside the lock. No luck there. He twisted it to the left. No luck there, either. Finally, in sheer desperation, he twisted the blade to the right. He could hear footsteps coming in his direction.

The lock clicked and the door opened on its hinges. Wasting no time, Lysander seized the amulet and bolted to the door fast as a streak of light. He did not much care anymore if they all heard him. Let them come if they wanted: they would not stop him.

He climbed quickly and easily out of the window and ran off across the snowy grounds. A large gate surrounded the mansion, about a hundred yards away on each side, twelve feet tall. Stopping just short of it, Lysander threw the pendant on the ground and stomped on it over and over with his boot. Nothing happened. He took out his penknife and jabbed the blade deep into the faceted yellow crystal. As he did so, a blinding light was emitted, and when he withdrew his knife the light dimmed to reveal that the crystal had been cut in half.

Smiling to himself, he picked up the halves. He looked up and noticed a small brook flowing through the frozen earth just beyond the fence at the back end of the mansion. He took several long strides forward, until he was within fifty yards of the fence, and threw the mutilated amulet with all his strength. It sailed over the fence and landed with a soft splash in the slow-moving water.

"That was for you, Arania," he said fiercely.

Just then a loud shriek which rendered enhanced hearing quite unnecessary pierced the stillness of the night. "The Amulet! *Where is the amulet of Amadyn?! It has been stolen from us, brethren!!!*"

Move, Lysander silently implored his paralyzed legs. *Move! He must not know it was me!* But he could not move an inch: weighed down as he was by his own dread.

Morugan`s footsteps were fast approaching: he would be at the door within seconds. Lysander looked up at the fence and knew what he had to do. He took a deep breath and started running for the fence as fast as he could, churning up great clouds of snow with his feet.

Twenty-five meters... Ten meters... Now five.. Two... One....

The youth reached out his hands to grab the tall stone walls, ready to climb up over them and run to freedom. But no sooner had he touched them than he felt a horrible pain, faster and fiercer than an electric shock, coursing through his entire body. He could not free his hands from the stone: they appeared to be glued to the large bricks.

Finally, with a loud grunt and an almighty wrench, he managed to pull his hands free. Immediately he collapsed onto the snow, nearly lifeless.

"Who is out there?" called the Head Vampire. "Who dares to disturb us?" He opened the door and saw the boy, lying near death at the foot of the great fence he himself had built, after all his hard work and careful planning.

He could not help but laugh. "He tried to escape. He tried to climb the fence. The fool, did he not know that the stone was imbued with a curse?"

Grovanitch had sidled up beside his master. "Is he dead, my lord? By all means he is no loss."

"No," replied Morugan. An evil smile curved over his fanged mouth. "He is not dead; the curse is not strong enough for that. He has merely been stunned. But I do not doubt that he will not try to escape again, now that he has seen the penalty for it."

"Indeed." Both vampires began to laugh, and then launched themselves skyward. They hovered over to the incapacitated young man, and Morugan quickly muttered a spell. At once, long black, shining ropes appeared, twisting themselves around Lysander's arms and legs, binding him tightly.

The crushing pressure roused him. Looking up at the two evil faces above his, Lysander was filled with more hatred than he had ever felt in his life.

"Let me go! Let me go, you sons of bitches! You can't do this to me!"

"SILENCE!" Morugan roared, and with a wave of his hand the youth stopped thrashing.

"You are mine now," hissed Morugan, his red eyes burning with rage. "MINE, do you hear me? And you will never leave! NEVER!"

He gestured with his arm, and Lysander disappeared and rematerialized inside his lonely prison. He raised tired, defeated eyes to the first pale rays of sunlight cresting over the horizon. He knew Morugan was right. He was a vampire now, and he belonged to the Head Vampire, to the clan. They were his family now.

This was not the end of it, either. Although he did not know it at the time, an ancient magic imbued the gemstone which he believed destroyed forever. He did not know that it would mend itself, float downstream until it reached the ocean, sailed onward farther and farther East until it came to America, a place he never dreamed he would see. He did not know that it would wash ashore and lay abandoned in an old seaside mineshaft for more than a century until it would be found by someone he never dreamed he would meet, living in a time he never dreamed he would see.

Anna Harper

A girl for whom he would soon find himself risking his own life.

III
Surprises In The Moonlight
New York, New York:
Autumn 1995

"Anna! Anna, are you listening?"

The Algebra teacher's whiney voice jolted Anna Harper out of her reverie. She had been staring morosely at the clock above the classroom door, unable to concentrate. Negative slopes were *such* a waste of time.

"Huh?" Her gaze drifted over to Mr. Angler, who eyed her impatiently from his desk through his square, black-framed glasses.

He sighed. "You might know the answer if you paid attention once in awhile. Does anyone else have an idea?"

"Well, maybe she just doesn't want to answer your stupid questions," Jennifer Mendez, Anna's best, and pretty much only, friend muttered under her breath.

The teacher's wrathful gaze deftly swiveled to her. "What was that, Ms. Mendez? Another of your cheeky remarks, I don't doubt. Detention tomorrow afternoon, young lady, and I don't want to hear a word about it."

Jennifer glared at him from her seat.

"I can't believe it," Jennifer groaned as the two girls walked home an hour later. "My mom is gonna kill me, this is the second week straight! And I told her I was going to put in more hours at Thali's." Thali's was the name of the pizza shop owned by Jennifer's parents where she worked three days a week.

"Yeah, well, maybe you should tone it down a little," Anna suggested, not really listening to her friend's tirade.

"It *was* toned down. For me." Jennifer's pale gray eyes sparkled. She had quite a mischievous streak and loved to frustrate hopelessly vapid teachers, like Angler. "Anyway," She turned to her friend, and her face became concerned. "What's wrong with you, Anna? You look ready to drop dead." It was true, Anna's face was pale and dark circles ringed her emerald-green eyes.

"It's nothing," Anna said dismissively, shoving a lock of her sandy-blond hair behind her shoulder. "I just haven't been sleeping real well lately."

"Right," replied Jennifer, who knew when Anna was lying and did not believe this story at all. "Look, I gotta be getting home. Call me later, okay?"

"Sure."

"You're coming to the mall tomorrow night, aren't you?" Jennifer smiled in a way that was more desperate than hopeful; her fifteenth birthday was the following weekend, and Anna was rarely allowed to go out on school nights.

"I'll see what I can do. I'll have to talk to Aunt Dianne. See you tomorrow, Jen." And with that she turned the corner and went on home alone.

What was the matter with her? She wondered. For days now she had been feeling strange, as though something was watching her. Something ancient and powerful and indescribably evil. She couldn't say what, exactly, and this was perhaps the most frightening thing of all. But she quickly shoved that thought out of her mind. She knew perfectly well that there were no such things as witches or werewolves, and she really did not need Jennifer thinking she was weird when everyone else at school probably did.

At fourteen years old Anna had moved more than most people do in thirty years. Her father was a professor of literature and folklore, and traveled extensively to gather information. She had never had time, or the precociousness to make friends, and when her mother died three years earlier the already quiet girl had become even more withdrawn. And all this notwithstanding, the late October afternoon was already beginning to get cold and dark. Sighing, Anna stepped up her pace. As she waited for the light at the intersection to change she noticed the great multitude of bats swarming past the late afternoon sun, blocking the light.

"What the hell?" she muttered. "I must be going crazy." She shook her head in annoyance and continued homeward.

"Anna Harper, where have you been?" her aunt demanded the moment Anna entered the house. Aunt Dianne was her mother's sister, but two women could not have been more different. Mrs. Harper had been kind and understanding, whereas Aunt Dianne seemed to speak only to complain and criticize.

Anna sighed. "I just met up with Jennifer for a few minutes. She wants to know if I can go to the mall tomorrow night."

"Absolutely not. Tomorrow is a school night."

"Friday is her birthday, and she always goes out with her family for her birthday," Anna protested. "This is my only chance to get her a present."

"Okay, fine. But you'd better have your homework done beforehand. I want you home by nine, and go straight to bed."

"Yes."

Anna opened her algebra textbook and scratched out a few problems while her aunt stirred a pot of soup on the stove. After a few moments of silence, she said, "In any case, you missed a phone call from your father because you dawdled. He's coming to the house this weekend."

"Dad's coming home?" Anna asked excitedly. She hadn't seen her father in eighteen months, not since his last business trip had begun.

"It's high time you had a stable home for once," he had said.

"For a few weeks," said her aunt. "Now, help me clear the table, the soup is ready."

The night watchman at Central Park never saw it coming. His mind went blank, his eyes glassed over, and he collapsed.

"Foolish human," A voice that cracked like a bolt of electricity called out happily. "This is our hour."

Morugan stepped out of the shadows. After living several centuries the vampire was not as quick as he had once been, although his power to hypnotize was as strong as ever. Now he bent over his prey and began to drink.

"Lysander," he called out when he had had his fill, "Come and eat, that you may be strong. The night wanes."

"I`m not hungry just now, Uncle." A young man watched from the cover of the trees but did not join in. In stark contrast to Morugan, Lysander Heistad looked nothing out of the ordinary, but Morugan knew that the youth`s senses were as finely tuned as a cat`s. He was strong and agile, and would make a fearsome hunter, the elder grudgingly acknowledged, if he were not so peculiar. Lysander tended to spend far more time alone than was customary for a vampire, and he showed little inclination for their way of life.

Morugan`s ruby-red eyes studied his surrogate nephew suspiciously. "We have not seen sustenance for nearly a fortnight. You are a strange one, Lysander, very strange indeed. Any other vampire would regard his clan as his topmost priority, and would do everything in his power to ensure their wellfare. I do not think I need to remind you of the consequences of insubordination."

"Yes, Uncle."

"Well, then, now that you are finally paying attention, I have some important news. I have felt that the Crystal of Amadyn is nearby, and I fully intend to retrieve it." He snorted. "No doubt it has fallen into the hands of some pathetic mortal, again. It hardly seems worth the effort to bother trapping them."

"You believe it is here?" Lysander asked, trying with all his might not to betray the spasm of fear that was shooting through him at exactly that moment. In over one hundred years Morugan had never once suspected that it had been he who had tried to dispose of the crystal. He had believed it stolen by a mortal, and Lysander himself had witnessed the carnage Morugan had inflicted upon an entire village of innocent human beings when he had found out that it was gone. And now, after all that needless suffering, the damn thing was back to haunt him again. How would Morugan punish him when he found out the truth? And more disturbing, how many innocent lives would be snuffed out this time around? A thousand, or more? Would the nightmare never end?

"Without a doubt," his uncle said, smiling a horrible fanged smile. "And this time we will be able to harness its ability to reverse our curse of being forever trapped in darkness. Just think of it, boy, no more cowering from the sunlight ever again. No more sneaking around in the dusk. We will finally be able to take what is ours."

Lysander said nothing, trying to keep his face as impassive as possible. He did not trust himself to speak.

"Hey, let's see what's in stock at Giridali's," Jennifer suggested at the mall the next evening. "I found the cutest bracelet there a few weeks ago."

"Correction," Anna chided her friend. "You want to see if Damien Roberson is in stock." Anna had met the tall, lanky blond boy within a few weeks of moving to New York, and she knew Jennifer was into him.

"So?" Jennifer demanded as they entered the store. "What's wrong with that?"

"What's wrong with what?" asked a cool voice, and the slim, attractive redhead turned around and immediately flushed pink.

"Nothing. How's work been going?"

"We've had twenty customers in two hours, that's a record," Damien cracked. "What's up, Anna?" He grinned at the pretty blond girl.

"My dad's coming home," Anna said. Damien knew what her father did; he was one of the few people she trusted enough to tell him about it.

"Where's he been?"

"Romania. He`s been doing a history of Vlad the Impaler."

"The original Dracula," Jennifer muttered, rolling her eyes. "I can`t believe people buy that crap."

"It`s true," Damien interjected. "My grandparents are from Romania, they know all about it."

"All about the myths, maybe. Well, Anna doesn`t believe it. Right, Anna?" Jennifer turned to her friend.

"Hmm?" Anna mumbled distractedly, rooting through the jewelry selection. "No, of course not." She continued to rummage, pushing aside a pair of red hoop earrings, a rhinestone studded tennis bracelet, and a bunch of plastic rings. "Come on, Damien, don`t you have anything better than...?"

But she never finished the question, because at that moment her hand closed around a slender silver chain. She lifted it up and found herself looking at a sun-yellow crystal, about the size of a strawberry, set in silver filigree. It gleamed brilliantly under the light, and Anna`s breath caught when she saw it.

"That`s really pretty, Anna. Looks like it cost a fortune."

Damien laughed. "How about $15? It`s nothing great as far as I know."

"Okay." Anna handed him the money.

"He likes you, Anna," Jennifer ragged her friend as they walked to the food court.

Now it was Anna's turn to blush. "He does not!"

"Oh, come on, don't tell me you didn't see the way he was looking at you." They bought milkshakes and took a seat at the nearest table. "So your dad's coming back. You must be exited."

"Yeah. I'm sick of Aunt Dianne bossing me around." Anna sighed. "I miss him, Jen."

"You're not going to leave, are you? Go with him like you used to?"

"I don't know," Anna said. "It's good that I've been able to get used to one place. But I don't want to be, you know, the weird professor's kid."

"You're *not* weird," Jennifer insisted. "You're just too quiet, that's all."

"Yeah, yeah." Anna shrugged. "I guess New York really isn't too bad." She finished her shake and stood up. "Come on, your mom is probably waiting for us."

"I'm coming." Jennifer followed Anna to the doors.

Later that night Anna sat up in her room looking at the crystal. Beautiful though it was, there was something about it that she did not like. Something strange and eerie. Like it was somehow connected to whoever or whatever had been making her so nervous. She couldn't help wishing that she had left the gem at the store. With a sigh, she tossed it into her desk drawer.

She needed to think about something else, anything else. So she picked up a pencil and the small notebook in which she wrote poems, a talent inherited from her mother, who had been a celebrated author of children's verse.

She scratched out a few sentences, then paused to admire her work. She loved how the words flowed together to say exactly what she wanted them to say.

"Anna!" Aunt Dianne called out from downstairs. "You'd better be sleeping!"

Anna sighed. "Okay!" Never mind, she could continue her poem tomorrow before school. She put the journal on the dresser, turned out the light, and crawled under the covers.

Lysander entered the room a few minutes later, acknowledging, somewhere in the back of his mind, he must be mad. Why was he here, doing Morugan's bidding like an obedient hound? He hated Morugan! Hated him with every fiber of his being!

He knew that this was where the gemstone was. He could feel it pulsing like a heartbeat. Silently as a specter, he walked over to the polished black dresser and pulled out the topmost drawer. There, lying in a tangled mass of chain, was the object that had haunted him for more than a century. The object that had caused him nothing but sorrow. He did not want to touch it. But, before he knew it, the thing was in his hand, flashing a steady pulse of yellow light. He pocketed it, little though he wanted to, and that was when he saw her. Anna Harper. Sleeping soundly not even ten feet from him. He inhaled a sharp intake of breath, and approached.

She was a beautiful child, one of the most beautiful he had ever seen. Her thick, honey-gold hair fell past her shoulders in delicate ringlets. Her skin was pearly white, and shone in the slats of moonlight that came in through the window. Her delicate features were completely content. If she only knew what danger she was in, because of that damnable object in his pocket! He pitied her, truly pitied her. So innocent and beautiful.

Goddamn it. *Goddamn it!*

But even though Lysander despised using humans as a source of sustenance, he knew his uncle's warning rang true. Besides, he could not go on much longer without a fresh supply of blood; weakness was creeping up on him. With a morose sigh he brushed her sand-colored hair off her neck and bent over her, fangs bared.

At that moment, however, his senses returned. He was not a cruel fiend like his uncle. He had never bitten a human before, and he did not intend to start. Besides, he sensed that this girl had a good heart and a trusting mind. Something Morugan would never have seen. How old was she? Fourteen, perhaps? The same age Arania had been when she died.

No, he would not do it.

"What's the matter with me?" he muttered in his native language. "It would be unforgivable to take your life for mine." His hand graced her face gently, and it pleased him to see that she did not cringe at his touch. He would find sustenance another way, it did not matter. Then he stood and walked back to the dresser, where he replaced the crystal.

Lysander knew that his uncle and the rest of the clan would flock to the spot now that he had revealed the gem. They would trick this child into giving it to them, and then kill the girl to keep their secret, just as they had so many times before. There was only one thing to do; lie to his uncle again. Morugan would eventually find out the truth and kill him, he knew, but it would be worth his death if she remained safe. He only hoped the girl would have a protector by then. He was tired of hiding his true self. Tired of being pushed around.

"I'll not be your slave, Morugan," he hissed fiercely in his native language, and he shoved the drawer closed. "Damned despot." Then he left and stormed back to his hideout in Central Park, his eyes taking on a fearful red gleam as his rage mounted.

Anna sat up in bed, shaking. She looked around the room; there was no sign of entry, and nothing appeared to be missing. But what was that voice she had heard? It wasn't anyone she recognized. Had she dreamed it?

Must have, she thought, feeling her rapid heartbeat begin to slow. Still, she decided to go for a walk to calm herself, like she did whenever she felt jittery. She crept silently past her aunt's room, out the door, and into the night.

It was chilly, but Anna didn't notice. She was too happy to be out, away from Aunt Dianne, amid the bats and owls and other creatures of the night.

Happy, she thought. *There's a word I haven't used in awhile.*

Before she knew it she was in Central Park, her favorite hiding place place. Anna loved its lush plants and beautiful blossoms, so different from the rest of the city.

When Dad comes, this is the first place we'll go, she vowed to herself.

She stopped to catch her breath at a rosebush, and two fireflies landed in her hand.

"Hello, fellas," she said happily, watching them walk up her fingers. "I guess you feel restless tonight, too."

The insects buzzed loudly, then flew off. Anna watched them go, then realized she was looking at something else. Something horrible.

A pair of glowing red eyes was staring at her from the darkness. She tried to turn away, but couldn't move an inch. The menacing eyes seemed to be sapping her energy, drawing her in. That was the last thing Anna saw before her world went black.

Lysander suddenly became aware of the girl collapsed before him and realized that he had, unintentionally, hypnotized her. Put her under a dangerous, sometimes irreversible, catatonic trance.

"No," he shouted, running to her. "No!" He dropped down beside her and shook her shoulder. "Get up, don't be taken, get up!"

Suddenly the girl's eyes opened, blinked confusedly, and she sat up. "Who are you?" she asked, massaging her forehead, which was aching terribly.

"No," he cried out, turning from her. "Look away!"

"What?"

"Look away. I don't want it to happen again."

"What are you talking about?" Anna demanded impatiently.

Still not looking at her, the strange man sighed and said, "I hypnotized you. I didn't intend to, but I can't control it sometimes."

"Hypnotized me?"

"Yes. I'm a vampire. That's how we catch prey."

Anna looked at him intently. From what she could make out in the dim moonlight, he was tall and wiry with collar-length black hair and was dressed completely in black. He could have been anyone at all.

"This is insane," Anna muttered. "There's no such thing as..."

But then she remembered that unfamiliar voice she'd heard. It was his.

Well, she admitted to herself, *This explains why I've felt so freaked out lately.*

"Wait a minute, *you're* the one who came to my house. But I thought I dreamed it."

"That was no dream, my dear girl," The man said in regretful tones. "You should go home, you`re not safe out here."

"You mean because I found a vampire in Central Park? Hey, I don`t think so." Anna stepped up closer to him and placed a small hand in his black-gloved one. "You could`ve sucked me bone-dry, but you said you wouldn`t harm me. I believe that."

Her words quieted the storm of Lysander`s mind and calmed his nerves. Whoever this girl was, he could see that he had been right about her. And she was so courageous!

"Indeed, I did," he agreed, smiling, and he turned to face her at last. "Most would run at the sight of such a frightful beast as me."

He was younger than she had thought he would be, and handsome, with a friendly, olive-skinned face and eyes that were not red at all but a deep, warm brown. His smile was dazzling. Anna thought she had never seen anyone who resembled a vampire less.

"You`re not too frightful," she remarked, laughing. "What`s your name?"

"Lysander."

"I`m Anna."

"The hour is late, Anna," Lysander said. "It`s high time you were back home."

Anna shrugged. "I can walk. It`s only a few blocks."

"I know a faster way."

"How?"

"Trust me." He took her hand. Before the girl could blink they were flying up over the trees, over the buildings.

"Wow!" Anna exclaimed. "Lysander, this is amazing."

"It`s a small restitution for the life I lead. The night can be filled with wonders, but it fast becomes a trap to those who cannot step out into the sun."

"Were you ever, you know, like I am?"

"Once. A long time ago. All vampires start out as humans, we`re not born."

"But you were bitten, weren't you?" Anna asked tentatively.

"Yes. A flock of the undead ensnared me with their hypnosis, just as you were hypnotized tonight. Before I knew it the damage was done, and I was condemned to this marginal existence, forced to hide from the sun and feed off the blood of mortal creatures. I never saw my family again," The young vampire added softly.

"I`m kind of cut off from people, too," Anna admitted. "You see, my father is a professor of literature and folklore, and he travels all the time to get information for his archives. We never stay anywhere longer than a few months, so I`m always the weird new kid."

"Surely you must have some friends."

She shook her head. "Not many. I guess I was just too shy." They landed in front of her house, and she said, "Seems like it was a lucky thing I couldn`t sleep tonight after all."

"Indeed." He grinned at her. "So you forgive me for the hypnotizing?"

"Yes." Anna laughed. "Good night." She walked into the house, shutting the door silently behind her.

"Good night, Anna," he said, watching her go.

The next day Anna got up feeling happier than she had in weeks, and went downstairs whistling.

"What are you so happy about?" Aunt Dianne grumbled between bites of rye toast.

"Nothing," Anna said, rinsing her cereal bowl out in the sink."Nothing. I just am. Nothing wrong with that, is there?"

"Don't be smart. And come right home after school to help me start cleaning the house, I won't have your father come home to a hovel."

"Okay, okay." Anna gathered her homework and put it into her backpack.

"You know, Anna, you can't pay the bills with a cheery disposition."

"I know." Anna said placidly. "Makes life a little easier to get through, though." And she walked out the door, whistling.

"Hmph," muttered her aunt as she turned a page in her newspaper.

That day at school Anna contributed much more than usual in class, volunteered to take attendance, and even answered yes to a note from Damien Roberson that Jennifer gave her, asking to go out on Saturday night. The plan was to go to Demacio's, a diner and dance club Anna loved.

"But will your aunt let you go?" Jennifer asked as they went through the lunch line.

"She let me go to the mall on Tuesday, didn`t she?" Anna retorted. "Besides, it`ll be easier to convince Dad."

"Well, at least one of us will be free this weekend," Jennifer groused. "I`m going to be buried in orders at Thali`s."

"Well, don`t forget to study for Angler`s algebra test next week," Anna chided as she placed a ham and cheese sandwich and an apple on her plate.

"Ha, ha, ha, very funny." Jennifer rolled her eyes as she spooned salad onto her plate. The girls chose a vacant table next to the doors. "Anyway, what`s up with you, Anna? You`ve been acting like a completely different person."

Anna shrugged. "I was just thinking about what you said. You`re right, Jen. I`ll never be happy anywhere unless I let people in."

Jennifer laughed. "Glad to see you finally realize it. I told you, there`s nothing wrong with you."

I can`t wait until Saturday, Anna thought, grinning at her friend.

It well past Midnight when the 365 Redeye from Boston prepared to go in for a landing.

"Please fold in your trays and put your seats into the upright position," The flight attendant announced. "We will be landing in John F. Kennedy airport in ten minutes."

The passengers folded in their trays and straightened their seats. But one little boy sat motionless, rigid with fear.

"Mommy, there`s a monster outside the plane." He gripped his toy truck tightly.

"There are no such things as monsters," his mother sighed.

"It`s true. I saw him right outside my window."

"What did he look like?"

"He was tall and thin, and he had white skin and red eyes. He was so scary."

"Well, he won`t be able to get in here." The young mother leaned over and kissed her son on the forehead. "Now put away your truck, we`re going to be landing soon."

"Okay." The little boy put his toy truck into his mother's backpack. "I can't wait to see Grandma and Grandpa."

"They'll be very happy to see you," His mother said, pleased that he had forgotten such nonsense as monsters for the time being.

All of a sudden there was a hard jolt that sent luggage spilling into the aisles.

"What was that?" the little boy cried out in a terrified whisper.

"Probably just a strong updraft," His mother said as the flight attendant announced that the plane was experiencing turbulence and asked everyone to fasten their seatbelts.

"I want to get off!" The little boy started crying.

His mother tried to silence him. "Don't cry, we'll be fine."

Just then another hard jolt caused a dinner trolly to careen down he aisle and smash at the other end, then a third knocked out the lights. Then the plane started to fall.

In the cockpit, the pilot was frantically trying to regain control. "I can't steady it," he shouted. "We're going down!"

"What the hell is going on here?" The co pilot looked out the window, and the last thing he saw before the plane crashed in a field was the horrible white face smiling a grotesque fanged smile at him through the window.

"Fools!" Morugan shrieked delightedly, his ruby-colored eyes flashing. He landed gracefully beside the cockpit door and wretched it open.

"We have done well tonight," said another vampire from Morugan's small local clan. "This will feed the clan for an entire moon cycle!"

"Quite," agreed another vampire, a haggard-faced woman with long, red curls. "But Master, where is that interesting nephew of yours? I thought we were expecting him."

"A stranger young one I have never seen," The first agreed. "Mark me; he will be trouble to us yet." The others murmured their agreement.

"Friends," Morugan said at last, "Do not be concerned. I sense that he merely lacks direction. And should anyone in this clan prove to be a trouble to us, remember that the pebble cannot fight the force of the ocean current that carries it." Then he pulled the pilot out of the cockpit, bared his fangs, and began to feed.

Suddenly a silver sword sailed through the air and stuck in the door of the cockpit. Morugan let out a furious hiss.

"Got you now, Bloodsuckers!" A haggard- looking man stepped forward, followed by six more. Sneering, they advanced upon the hissing, seething vampires.

"En guarde, Morugan!" He pointed his sword at Morugan. "Unless you're too afraid!"

Morugan drew his own sword and hit back the blow. "It is not yet daybreak, Garrison!"

Back and forth they fought, harder and harder.

Morugan sneered. "I say, you are almost too amusing for me to want to make an end of you."

"Ditto. It gets better and better."

Morugan began to chant in his native language, his eyes glowing brighter and brighter. The hunter flew back and hit a tree.

He got up shaking himself. "Now, what did I tell you last time about that hocus-pocus business?"

The Head Vampire cackled his ugly laugh. "I am one of the undead. You should know I am not to be trusted."

"Well, I got some tricks of my own!" The crystal the hunter wore around his neck, which was exactly like the Crystal of Amadyn but bright red-began to flash, and the Head Vampire cried out in anguish as the intense light began to scorch him. The rest of the clan gave a collective hiss of furry.

"Not so pompous now, are you, you repulsive son of a bitch?"

Morugan dropped to his knees, blinded by pain and rage.

"Master, dispose of the poacher!" one of the Vampires shouted as he struggled with another hunter.

"Shut up, you!" The hunter punched him fiercely.

Morugan struggled to his feet and muttered a hasty incantation in his own language, and a massive wall of fire suddenly erupted, surrounding Garrison. The Head Vampire advanced upon his most hated enemy, cackling.

Garrison drew his dagger and slashed at Morugan. "Back off, freak!"

A bloodless wound appeared in the Head Vampire's face. He uttered a low, warning growl, like that of an angry wolf. "Brazen mannerisms will not save your hide, Garrison," he said in a deadly hiss. Another incantation, and a deep wound appeared on Garrison's chest, and another on his leg. He sank to the dirt, with a groan.

The hunter merely grasped the crystal and muttered an incantation in medieval Latin. The gashes healed in mere moments. He quickly got to his feet and rounded on the master, intent on finishing what he had started.

"No one harms the master!" The young Ignatio came charging at Garrison, shrieking like an enraged bat. He began to mutter a killing curse, but quick as a flash the hunter drove a wooden stake into his heart and summoned the power of his crystal. The vampire burned to a cinder within moments, as the gemstone derived its power from the sun itself. Seeing this, two more of the clan accosted the hunter, but they too were met with the same fate, one after the other.

Another hunter went after Morugan, who slashed at him, and he too fell dead. "Let us leave here, now!" he shouted to his clan-now reduced to four vampires. In an instant they were gone. Garrison and his men were left alone.

"I hate it when they do that," one of the hunters fumed. "I really hate it! How the living hell are we supposed to catch them?"

"That's just it," said another. "We can't."

"Never say never." Garrison pulled out laptop computer and typed in the password to a GPS system. "I figured they might try that old trick again. That's why I had this little feature installed." He honed in on the neighborhood of Manhattan, knowing that the vampires would not have gone far-his encounters with Morugan had taught him that the Head Vampire liked to go to roost well before daybreak. He studied the streets on the monitor. It was already nearly two in the morning, and he knew he couldn't kill the head vampire at night, when he was most powerful.

"Come on, come on," he muttered impatiently. He would not allow these creatures, who had destroyed thousands of families, his own among them, to escape. He had been hunting them since late adolescence, knew more about them than just about anyone else.

Finally a location on Westminster Alley caught his attention. The house was a fantastic mansion called Bluerock manor, an abandoned Le Rue that was ideal for infestation by such creatures. He was absolutely sure this was where the creatures had chosen to hide.

"We`ve found the place, boys. All we have to do now is wait for them to show themselves."

They burned the plane and deceased passengers, as was customary, then constructed a memorial tier.

"Jesus, look at this mess. You'd think they'd planned to hibernate for another two hundred years."

"Hey, how many of them were there tonight anyway? I thought there were eight. I counted seven, including the old crone."

Morugan, too, was having similar ideas. Upon arrival at Bluerock Manor, he looked around for his surrogate nephew. He desired a discussion pertaining to his absence tonight. Or more accurately, his absences *every*night. He would have almost believed the youth was not a vampire at all, had it not been he himself who had bitten Lysander. Most disturbing indeed.

Where was that boy?

"Lysander, come. I must speak with you now."

In a moment Lysander had appeared. "You summoned me?"

"I desire to know where you go off to every night. It is customary for the undead to work as one."

"I was here, Uncle," Lysander said, which was perfectly true. He had not left the mansion once tonight. He hoped his uncle would not ask why, he must not put himself in danger while Anna needed him.

Morugan said, "I will have you know, Lysander, that Garrison and his lot accosted us tonight. They have killed half of our number already. You are needed to safeguard our way of life from those bothersome poachers, and I fully expect you to participate from now on. Do not forget the warning given you."

"Lysander the freak," taunted Padmona. "You would think he was frightened of those pathetic mortals and their parlor tricks." She snickered.

"Well, at least I`ve got sense enough to fear, Padmona," Lysander said. And he sneered smugly, because Padmona could not deny it. She was terrified of death. She had given up her mortal nature to survive Consumption over a century earlier. His sister, in Lysander`s view, had been a much stronger woman to accept her fate as she had. Arania would never have made an evil covenant like that to save herself.

Padmona hissed furiously. "I will teach you to taunt me, wastrel!" Her luminous green eyes flared red.

"Enough!" shouted the Head Vampire. "We must be united, or we are sure to fail. Go now, both of you."

Lysander stalked off down the stairs, fuming. He had lived with the clan for one hundred and twenty years, one hundred and twenty long, dark years, and they still treated him like pond scum. It was grating to constantly be rebuked or sneered at. *I don`t care what Morugan says*, he fumed inwardly. *These monsters are not my family, and they never will be.*

Lysander kept walking until he reached the first floor of the mansion. Finally he went into a small room off the Armory.

The moment he stepped inside he began to feel less irritated. This was his own special haven within the mansion, or the Hellhole, as he privately referred to it. A lush Atrium dimly lit by torches, and supplied with many different plants. No one could find him here. Morugan himself did not even know about the Atrium. It was kept locked, and Lysander alone possessed a key. Had the others been able to see it, he knew, they would find the place laughable. To him, on the other hand, it brought comfort like nothing else could. It was calming to be amid familiar plants; Thyme, Chamomile, Aconite, as though they were old friends. Sometimes he though it was the one reason he had managed to retain his sanity all these years.

He looked out through the window at the moon and sighed. It was another beautiful night, one that Arania would never see, and he himself would never be able to enjoy. In fact, it was almost like the very night he had been attacked by Morugan and fainted, only to find himself in this hideous mansion. He remembered it all as though it had happened only days ago. The horrible pain at his neck as the Head Vampire had bitten him, the terror of being trapped inside that tiny room, and his failed attempt at escaping. The old scar at the side of his neck was barely visible these days, but he became dimly aware of a dull, pulsating ache at the spot.

"NO!" he howled in Romanian, bringing his fist thudding down onto a side table. "NO! I DON'T WANT IT!" He was tired of recalling that horrible time of his sister's death, his transformation into a creature he loathed. And he knew full well that it had been his own fault. If he had not been so foolish to venture out in the dead of night, coerced by grief and longing, he surely would never have met the Head Vampire. He would have never been bitten, never pushed aside and snubbed by those monsters.

Then, all of a sudden, the words spoken to him by the Head Vampire that night all those years ago came into his mind unbidden and unwanted.

Do not let thoughts of the past cloud your senses, boy. This is your home now.

Those words continued to ring in his ears now as he looked at the one small portrait of Arania he still had. And as much as Lysander hated to admit it, Morugan had offered sage advice. He was what he was, and there was no point in lamenting what could not be changed. All he could do was hold onto the purity of heart that had never deserted him, and watches over those like Anna Harper, who needed a protector.

"My dear sister," he said in his native language, looking into Arania's joyful face. "You wouldn't want me to give in to them. If only I could be as strong as you were, maybe you would have been proud of me."

He grinned slightly. "Well, perhaps you will be yet. It's not over."

The next day Anna saw the blue Pontiac in the driveway when she came home from school and gasped happily.

"Dad!"

He wasn't due home until Sunday. She careened into the house as fast as she could, past the living room and into the kitchen where her father was having coffee.

"Dad!"

Laughing, he caught her in a hug as she passed. "How's my favorite girl?"

"Great," Anna said. "You came home early."

"I didn't want to be away from you one day longer. So," he said as she took a seat beside him, "How's school been going?"

"Okay. Mr. Angler's class is pretty difficult, but I got an A on my last English report."

"Well, it's good to know we have something in common," Mr. Harper chuckled. "Good work, Anna."

"And," Anna waited until her aunt left the room to say it, "Damien Roberson asked me out for Saturday night, at eight."

"Who's Damien Roberson?"

"I told you about him. Jennifer introduced us, he works at Giridali's at the mall. We'll only be gone an hour or so."

"That sounds okay to me," Her father said, "No later than nine-thirty, okay? I'll come pick you up."

"Okay," she agreed. "So Dad, what did you find in Romania? That's where vampires come from, isn't it?"

"Their mythology traces back to ancient Romania, yes," he agreed. "But you do know that there are no such things as vampires, don't you?"

"Yes." Anna knew this wasn't the time to say that she had met a real vampire only days ago.

"Well," Mr. Harper began, "Over two thousand years ago an ancestor of Vlad the Impaler lived in what is now known as Dracula's Castle. His name was Amadyn, and his family was the wealthiest in the land. But Amadyn was lonely, and far from happy."

"Why was that?"

"Legend has it that Amadyn was a magician. Very powerful, but he could not always control his powers. His ability to hypnotize was particularly troublesome, especially when he was angry."

Just like Lysander, Anna thought.

"As he got older and more powerful he was held responsible for putting several people under irreversible trances, and was threatened with flogging and the gallows many times," Her father continued. "Then when Amadyn was twenty-three, he met and fell in love with Mariela, a beautiful young maidservant to his uncle. Unbeknownst to Amadyn's family, they courted for a few years until his father found out and disowned him. The young couple married and left Amadyn's childhood home for a small cottage several day's journey away. They lacked money and had to work very hard to survive, but they were happy. However, when Amadyn was barely thirty, his wife died giving birth to their first child. He was so overwhelmed by grief that he left his home and his son and wandered alone through the forest. He walked on for days, getting weaker and weaker, until he collapsed with exhaustion at the doorstep of a mansion called Blair's Manor."

"And vampires lived there?"

"In fact, they did," Mr. Harper said. "When he awoke he was surrounded by them."

"He must have been terrified."

"I don't doubt it. He was able to find the courage to fight, however, for several hours until the Head of the clan killed him. Drained the life right out of him. With the sorcerer dead the Head Vampire, Hierchan, created an amulet that would allow him and his followers to return no matter how many times they were killed off. All it took was for some unwitting mortal to touch it, and the vampires would appear. That was usually the first person they killed, to keep their existence a secret, you know. And what's worse is this particular gem, if exposed to the first rays of the sun after the full moon, would grant them the ability to walk in daylight."

"And that's what happened, wasn't it?"

"That's what the legend says. I heard that it was lost some hundred years ago when the vampires were last banished. But that's only mythology, remember."

"Interesting story," Anna said, recalling the crystal stashed in her room.

"Lysander, have you not found the holder of the crystal yet?" Morugan asked late that night. He paced the main hall of Bluerock Manor agitatedly.

Lysander said nothing right away. He knew he would have to think his answer through carefully before he gave it, or all was lost. Finally he said, "I don't know where to begin looking, Uncle. There are thousands of people in the city. I'm not as experienced a tracker as you."

"You are not working hard enough!" Morugan's eyes were particularly terrible to behold tonight. "Our survival depends upon our ability to catch prey and our willingness to improve our status in the hierarchy! Have I not told you this time and again?"

"Yes, Uncle. I understand."

Morugan's rant had not dissipated. "The hunters are fast on our tail," he raged. "If we do not control them they will overpower us, drive us away! The clan may not see sustenance for several moon cycles; it was all I could do to catch these tonight." And he swore in Romanian.

He thrust aside a partition and revealed two prostrate figures. The woman, sporting bloody puncture wounds on her neck, was clearly dead. However, there was also a child beside her, who was still breathing. A black-haired little girl. She was no more than eight years old, and heartbreakingly beautiful. Lysander was reminded forcibly of his sister: he swallowed the hard lump in his throat with difficulty.

"It takes only one weak link to break a chain forged of steel," Morugan warned his nephew. "I tell you now, Lysander, do not be that link. Fulfill your duties to this clan. Go and dispose of the mortal who possesses the stone, then bring it directly to me. Tonight. Oh, and do eat before you depart." And here the Head Vampire smirked. "I have taken the liberty of saving something for you." With that he was gone in a swirl of cloaks.

Lysander scowled at the place where his surrogate uncle had vanished. "I'll not obey you, damned monster," he hissed. His anger towards the whole clan was growing.

It was a moment before he remembered the injured child in the room with him. Forcing down his loathing for the clan, he knelt beside her and placed a hand to her chest. Her pulse was very weak; could he revive her? She was just so small. Delicate. He sighed sadly.

"Oh, child."

Suddenly, she opened her eyes and let out a gasp, of fear as well as pain. "Who are you?" Her right ankle was bent at an odd angle, and she was bleeding copiously from a gash on her arm. The smell of her blood hit him like heat from a furnace, and yet he found that he could easily ignore it. How strange.

"I'm here to help you," he said, quickly ripping a strip off of the lace tablecloth to his right, and tying it tightly around her arm like a tourniquet. "Don't try to move, I'll be right back."

He raced down the corridor to his secret Atrium and retrieved his satchel of medical supplies and herbs, then hurried back to the dungeon where the child lay.

Kneeling beside her, he examined the wound. "You'll need stitches, but it's not bleeding as badly now," he said, producing a jar that contained a solution of Lavender and Thyme from his satchel. "Here, this will help with the pain." He applied the solution to the site, and then began to sew the wound closed. "Just stay still. You're going to be fine."

As he said it, he could hear other words swirling around inside his head, words in his native language. They sounded like an enchantment.

What in the name of brimstone is going on here? He wondered. How very strange. He was utterly perplexed, but said nothing about it aloud, lest he should frighten the child. Her breathing was easier now, the fearful expression gone from her face.

"You're one of them," she stated, looking at him with something akin to wonder. "Why are you saving me? I'm bleeding like crazy."

At this moment, he looked into her eyes, and grief momentarily robbed him of breath: They were exactly like Arania`s eyes had been, large and round and pale blue with a narrow band of lightest gray encircling the pupils.

"I'm nothing like the others," he answered when he had found his voice again. "I don't kill, little one, I heal." He set to work bracing her ankle, and as he did so he felt her tiny body relax upon hearing these words.

"That's good to know."

"I'm Lysander," he offered, looking at her fondly. "What's your name?"

"Kari. Kari Holmes." And now her eyes were fluttering closed. He was fearful that she had lost too much blood.

"Stay with me, Kari," he urged, raising her head up. "Stay awake. I'll get you to a hospital soon."

"What-what about my mom?"

Lysander looked over at the dead woman beside them, and he felt horrible. The poor child was motherless, alone in the world.

"She's gone, sweetheart," he said gently. "I'm so sorry." He felt her tears soak his shirt as she wept bitterly. "Shh, it's all right." He cradled her head in his hands. "I will protect you, I promise."

After a few moments Kari wiped away her tears with the back of her hand. "I'm glad you're here, Lysander."

The night was cold as Lysander walked on with Kari in the protective circle of his arms. He talked to her to keep her awake, told her about his past life: His home and his family, and even about his lost sister.

"She died a few years ago," he said, thinking there was no need to mention that it had, in fact, been more than a century.

"Wh-what h-happened?" Kari asked. The little girl was shivering with cold, and he was trying to warm her by wrapping her in his jacket.

"She was very sick," he said, holding her close. "I couldn't help her, no one could."

"S-sorry to h-hear t-that."

He smiled as he wrapped her more snugly in the jacket. "You're my top priority now, Kari."

He looked around, and saw the hospital up ahead, its widows glowing with yellow light. He went inside quickly.

"Hello," said the receptionist behind the front desk. "What brings you here?"

"Her ankle is broken," Lysander explained, "and she's lost some blood, I think it's serious."

The receptionist nodded as she entered the information in the computer.

"She's lost her mother," he added. "They were ambushed."

The woman looked at him quizzically. "Are you her father?" The vampire had to fight not to laugh. What a question!

"No, I'm-just a friend."

The receptionist nodded. "Okay, what's her name?"

"Kari. Kari-Holmes. She's about eight years old, I think."

The woman frowned, but asked no more questions. She produced a plastic identification bracelet which she fastened around Kari's wrist. "Have a seat, we'll be ready for her in a moment."

"Thank you."

Lysander sat in one of the plastic waiting chairs, looking down at the gorgeous, barely-conscious child in his arms. *What's going to happen to you, little one?* He wondered. *Is there someone who could come for you?* He knew she would be safe only as long as she remained in the hospital, unless a relative could be reached. He cared nothing for himself, perilous though his own situation was. But the child must never come to harm. If only he could look after her himself.

Suddenly a voice called out, "Kari Holmes?" A nurse was approaching, pushing a gurney.

"Here." Lysander stood up. When the nurse stopped before them he laid his little friend down carefully on the gurney. "You'll be fine," he whispered to her, grasping her tiny hand in his.

"We'll send for you once we've gotten her settled," the nurse told him, and she wheeled Kari out, leaving the vampire to wait.

"Who do we have here?" the doctor asked when he entered the room.

"Eight-year-old female," the nurse reported. "Her right ankle is broken, and she's suffered significant blood loss."

The physician checked the name on Kari's identification bracelet. "Kari Holmes." He examined the wound on her arm. "Well, whoever stitched her up knew what they were doing, this is very well done." He propped open her left eyelid, then her right, shining a penlight into her eyes. "Kari? Can you hear me?"

"Yes." She squinted. "Ow, that's bright."

"Sorry." He clicked off the light, then took the girl's pulse. "She's responsive," he told the nurse, "but she'll need a transfusion. What's her blood type?"

The nurse consulted her notes. "She's AB Positive."

"Get me half a pint."

So the nurse left and returned with the blood five minutes later. The doctor put on a pair of latex gloves and prepped Kari's skinny arm with an alcohol swab.

"I need you to stay very still now," he told her. "This'll sting a little, but you'll feel better in awhile." He slid the needle into her arm, and although she had to grit her teeth to keep from crying out, she did not flinch. "Good girl." He secured the IV line with tape, and then attached a bag of painkillers as well.

Next they removed her clothes and dressed her in a hospital gown-they had to cut off her blue jeans because of her broken ankle-and the physician examined the fracture.

"It feels like the break is at the tibia."

"I can take her down to Radiology right now," the nurse offered, but he shook his head.

"No, we can't move her. We'll have to do it here."

So that is what they did. The nurse positioned Kari beneath the camera while the doctor lined up the shot.

"Okay, Kari, don't move." He snapped the picture. "Good girl." The nurse took the film to be developed, and in half an hour they were putting a proper cast on Kari's ankle.

The child yawned. "I'm so tired."

"I know," the nurse said kindly. "You can sleep in a moment, honey."

The girl's eyes closed. "'Kay."

Meanwhile in the waiting room, Lysander kept looking at the clock. Although he was immortal, he was getting anxious for news about Kari. What was taking so long? Finally, after almost two hours, the nurse who had taken Kari back returned.

"You can go and see your daughter now, the doctor's just finishing up examining her."

"She's not my daughter," said Lysander, "but I'm all she has."

The nurse looked at him quizzically. "What?"

He shook his head. "Never mind."

"This way." She led him down the hall to a patient room. "She's in here."

Inside Lysander found an older man with salt-and-pepper hair bent over Kari, the bell of his stethoscope to her chest. When he noticed the vampire, he straightened up and replaced the instrument around his neck.

"Mr. Holmes."

"Heistad," Lysander corrected, coming to Kari's side. "How is she?"

"Nothing plenty of rest won't cure," the doctor said, pinning an X ray to the lighted box on the wall. "Here's the fracture." He pointed to it with a pen. "It's a clean break, so it won't take long at all to heal. She did lose quite a lot of blood, but we gave her a transfusion. She's going to be fine, she's just very tired." He cast the vampire a curious look. "Were you the one who stitched up the wound?"

If it had been possible for Lysander to blush, his face would have turned brilliant crimson. He did not look at the physician. "Yes."

"I was wondering who did that. It saved her life, any worse and she would be dead by now."

You don't know the half of it, Lysander thought. He had to repress a shudder.

162

At that moment Kari's eyes opened. "Lysander."

"I'm here, Kari," he said, stroking her cheek. "I'm right here." She relaxed immediately at his touch.

"She's one lucky little girl," the physician commented. "to have such a loving friend."

"She's not mine," said the vampire gloomily. "I can't keep her safe."

"She's perfectly safe here." The doctor gave him the same uncomprehending look he had been getting all night.

"That's not what I mean." He sighed. "I mean, I won't be able to look after her when she's released. Protect her from getting hurt again."

"Do you know anyone who could come for her?"

Lysander shook his head. "I would take her if I could, but I can't."

Kari looked from one to the other of them, her eyes large and fearful.

"Get some sleep, honey," the doctor said to her. "We'll work something out." Smiling slightly, he left the room.

Kari grasped Lysander's hand. "Don't go. I'm scared."

"Don't be," he said, pulling the blanket more snugly around her. "I'm not going anywhere tonight." He stroked her hair, and she sighed with pleasure.

"Thank you."

He smiled at her. "Rest now, darling. No one will harm you."

Lysander sat at Kari's side all through the night, hating himself for having to leave her. If not for Morugan, none of this would have happened. He hated being a danger to mortals.

Finally at five-thirty in the morning, the doctor returned.

"We've just gotten a hold of her aunt," he said. "She's coming later this morning, and she says she'll arrange for Kari to stay there when she's released."

"Thank you," Lysander said. He turned to Kari, touched her arm, and she awoke.

"Kari? Kari, sweetheart, I need to be leaving now."

She looked at him apprehensively.

"Don't worry," he said gently. "They'll take good care of you here."

The doctor nodded. "We will, honey, I promise."

Kari reached out and laced her fingers between Lysander's. "Thank you, Lysander," she said. "Thank you for everything."

He smiled. "It was no trouble. Be safe, little one." And with that he left the hospital to find a place to hide: The sun would be up in less than an hour.

It was good to know that the frightened child had trusted him enough to allow him to help her, he thought. He liked that she saw him as a friend and not a vampire. But he still wondered if he would be strong enough to protect her and the thousands of others Morugan intended to slaughter.

First thing first, he thought as he sailed up over the clouds, out of sight of any mortals who would be out at this time of night: he must find out where these strange new abilities had come from. Perhaps a better understanding of what had happened to him would give him a better chance of making sure that when he met his death it would mean the end of Morugan as well... perhaps the library would have books to shed some light on the issue.

It would not be easy to get up there. His uncle's pet timber wolf liked to sleep outside the room. The creature strongly disliked him, and was bound to alert Morugan to his presence.

He snuck inside and listened hard. He could hear loud chattering from inside the drawing room. Morugan and Grovanitch. The two vampires appeared to be having an argument.

"You have entrusted him with the task of finding Amadyn's amulet?" Grovanitch was asking. "I cannot help but feel that this is an unwise decision, my lord. You know he has never exhibited even the remotest inclination towards our way of life."

"We must use him." This from Morugan. "He has the most finely tuned senses of us all. You forget, I was the one who bit him, the one who turned him. He heard me coming a mile away, even as a dull -witted human. He ran. I pursued. He was on the pathway out of the city when I finally caught up with him. I do not doubt that he very well might be a true asset."

At this Grovanitch hissed with indignation.

"Rubbish. That coward could not bring himself to harm a fly, much less a human."

"Do not say such things," said Morugan. "He is lacking in guidance that is all. We must simply teach him that such roguish behavior is not acceptable. He must be honed; he must use his ancestry to aid in our struggle."

"Ancestry? Of what are you speaking, Master? A vampire is not born, he is created."

"He is the descendant of Amadyn. The most powerful magician for over a thousand years, as you well know, you old fool." Morugan`s voice held a definite note of disgust.

Lysander gasped. Him! Descended from Amadyn! So he really had been doing magic when he was taking care of little Kari. Those strange words in his mind had really alleviated her pain. He was an even more powerful healer than he had realized. He strained his ears harder.

"Amadyn? Are you quite sure?"

"I am not mistaken," said Morugan churlishly. "The boy undoubtedly recalls Amadyn`s might, as did all those of his line who preceded him, you have only to look carefully at him. It is true that their abilities have diminished over the years. However, he seems to have inherited Amadyn`s abilities in full measure."

It was all Lysander could do not to fall over in shock. Full measure! So an end to this nightmare was possible after all.

"So you believe he is a threat? Against all of us together?" Grovanich snorted derisively. "Master, you of anyone should know that conformity builds strength. He is but one. He would be a fool to turn on us, an utter fool, half-wizard or not. You yourself said it; a pebble cannot fight the current of the ocean. The wind cannot make a mountain bend to its will."

"Indeed, no." The Head Vampire was smirking. "He lacks the control to be as powerful as he could be. He lets his heart overwhelm him, cloud his decisions, and therein lies his greatest weakness."

Anger flashed white-hot inside of Lysander. Did they truly believe him weak simply because he did not engage in their refined form of cruelty? Well, he would simply have to prove them wrong.

IV
A New Reason To Hope

He stormed through the ornate entrance hall and up the wide stone staircase, growing more furious with every step. He reached the second floor, and walked over to the much narrower, twisting staircase that led up to the tower.

Wresting a torch out of its bracket, he began his ascent through the dark stairwell.

Morugan had refined his powers, so therefore he must have spell books lying about. He must get hold of them, must practice and refine his own abilities, he thought, as a large Black Widow spider scuttled out of a crack in the walls and ran past his feet.

He looked out the window. The moon was high and full; he would have mere hours to set to work before daybreak.

Finally he reached the landing at the top of the tower. As he had suspected, the wolf lay supine across the door. As the vampire approached, it opened one eerie yellow eye and growled softly.

"It figures," groaned Lysander. "Is there really nothing better for you to do than snap at me day after day?"

The wolf snapped at his ankle, and he shook it loose. "Get off; I've got work to do tonight."

The wolf growled louder and backed away, keeping its luminous eyes on him. Lysander ignored it and opened the door.

He proceeded into the library, the small, circular room in the highest turret. He placed the torch into the bracket by the door, and walked over to the nearest bookshelf.

There were books stacked from the floor to the ceiling, books on every imaginable subject. The young vampire peered at them closely. He saw several useful books, volumes on magical plants-no doubt used by Morugan to create poisons- volumes on hypnotism- he must read this and find out if he might not learn to control it-books on dueling with magic- it was no good telling himself that he was physically stronger than Morugan, for the Head Vampire was sure to fight unfairly- and many more.

Lysander pulled out the books on dueling first. Morugan`s snide remarks were still burning in his ears. He sat himself down on the floor and opened the topmost one, entitled *Basics of Dueling*, and began to read.

"The practice of dueling by magical means is an exercise in both mental and physical focus. Therefore, this volume begins with learning to master one`s thoughts and emotions..."

Control of his thoughts and emotions....well, he had managed that easily enough tonight in the presence of an injured and terrified eight-year-old child, but he knew it would be much more difficult to do in front of Morugan. He kept reading...

"Eye contact is essential, for the eyes are the window to the mind...." He found himself thinking about Anna: her sweet smile, her gentle voice, and her brilliant green eyes that reminded him of the beautiful, sun-filled fields his family had owned in Bucharest-how he would have loved to be back there. He wondered if he would ever see the girl again.

Focus, you fool, focus! he snapped at himself.

He continued reading. After another forty-five minutes he closed the book and started practicing a simple Summoning spell. He looked at the book of magical plants on the shelf and, focusing hard, muttered the enchantment.

The book twitched feebly between its neighbors, but did not leave the shelf. This would be harder than he thought.

Gritting his teeth, he tried again. This time the small book fell to the ground.

"Oh, come off it," the vampire said irritably. "That was a clear order."

He would simply have to try again. He glared at the book, feeling a hot energy coursing through him.

It lifted up off the ground and sailed slowly towards him. Smiling with satisfaction he stood up and caught it in his outstretched hand.

"Now we're getting somewhere."

He continued to practice, over and over, making things zoom across the room. Every time they came faster and faster, and soon he was moving objects much larger than books.

Finally, after he had been there longer than he knew, he stopped and looked out the window. The sky was beginning to lighten; he would have to stop.

The next chapter was on striking opponents. He would have to remember to look at that tomorrow night.

"Until next evening, then," he said, picking up the candle. But before he left he glared at a volume on treating magical wounds and ailments. He wanted to make sure that he would be able to keep fighting until the very last, no matter what Morugan did to him.

Lysander went swiftly and silently back down the stairs, past the Ballroom, and back down the corridors to his Atrium. Sitting at the small table at the right hand corner, he pulled Arania`s portrait towards himself.

"Arania, it`s a miracle," he said excitedly in Romanian. "I might finally have found a way to stop that demon that separated us. We'll be together again soon, I promise you."

The next evening Lysander went directly to the library in the top turret and opened the dueling book, which was marked exactly in the place where he had left off the night before. He began to read...

"All magical beings have their own ways of inflicting damage upon their enemies. However, the greatest duelists have one thing in common; the knowledge that they must embrace their motives. They must have an unrelenting desire to inflict damage."

Well, he didn't think embracing his motives would be a problem, it was exactly the opposite of that which worried him. He had never been a killer, and if he was to start now, he would have to remember to draw a line between innocent and guilty. He must keep Anna away from this place, away from Morugan.

"As in the simpler forms of magic, eye contact is crucial between combatants. Merely saying the enchantments is not enough."

He wondered fleetingly if Morugan had ever felt afraid of his own power, that he could not control himself, and for the first time in what seemed like an eternity, he smiled. It seemed absurd, even to his own ears.

"The curses one magical being might inflict on another are many and varied. The most elementary might be deflected, but there are those whose effects cannot be easily fought. Therefore vigilance is always needed."

Too right it is, Lysander thought dryly. Well, he would just have to be cautious, that was all. Keep Morugan guessing for as long as possible.

Finally he decided to try it. Closing his eyes tightly he imagined the fight, the feeling of finally striking at the one who had taken him from the life he knew and reduced him to a pathetic creature cowering in the shadows.

Heat rose up inside him, right behind his eyes, and before he knew it he had melted the metal ladder used to access the topmost books right in half simply by glaring at it.

"Amazing!" he whispered out in Romanian, "Absolutely amazing!"

Time to see if he could melt it completely. He focused harder, glaring at the ladder until his head was throbbing, and he melted the ladder into an amorphous blob.

"Come out and fight then, Morugan," he sneered. "Come out and give me all you've got. You can't beat me."

He continued practicing over and over again until the headaches were unbearable. By the time the sky had begun to lighten, he was able to reduce just about any object to a molten mess. Exhausted, he went back to his atrium, sore but filled with pride. Anna would be safe. There was no way he wouldn't be able to take out the Head Vampire now.

The next few nights passed in much the same way. By the time a week had passed, he was reading books on healing enchantments and magical plants, and he had begun to learn teleportation, which he had never dreamed he would be able to do.

"The important thing to remember when you are teleporting," The book repeatedly stressed, *"is that you must always have a clear view of the location where you*

want to go. As in all branches of magic, there is nothing more critical than remembering your determination to emerge there. A complete mastery of all elements is essential."

This was proving to be a much more difficult task to accomplish than anything he had attempted to do before. But he had continued practicing, hour after hour, day after day.

On Saturday night he went up to the topmost turret of Bluerock Manor and locked the door behind him.

He closed his eyes tight and pictured the place where he wanted to go. The hidden glade in Central Park. He muttered the enchantment, and within two seconds he was there.

Unfortunately, Garrison was at this precise moment standing right in front of his computer. He had been watching and waiting, for over a week, for some sign of magical activity, something to tell him where the vampires had gone to. And now he knew his guess had been right on par all along. This one act had finally been powerfully magical enough to register on the screen.

"We've got them! We've got them now!" he shouted to his men.

"Are you serious?" one asked.

"Morugan?"

"That's impossible. He wouldn't be so careless when he knows we're around."

"Well, whoever it is, they're mine," Garrison said firmly. "I want the rest of you to stay here; I'll deal with it on my own."

Lysander was, at the moment, completely unaware of any such impending trouble. He was busily perusing his book of magical herbs and scanning the forest floor for signs of them. He had gathered a great bundle of them when all of a sudden he found himself hurtling headlong into a tree trunk.

Breathing hard, he looked around and spotted his assailant, who he recognized as none other than Herald Garrison.

"So, thought you were too smart to be trailed, did you?" The vampire hunter kicked him hard. "Well, I've got some questions for you." He punched the vampire hard in the face, and then muttered a stinging spell that sent the vampire doubling over. "And you'd better give me the right answer, or you'll really regret it, you freak."

Meanwhile, across town, Anna slid nervously into a booth opposite Damien at Demacio's.

"I'm really glad you agreed to this, Anna," He said, his blue eyes gleaming. "I've been wanting to ask you out for forever."

"For real?" Anna couldn't believe her ears.

"Yeah. You really need to believe that you're better than a dime a dozen, 'cause you are. I know I'm not the first person to tell you that."

"Believe me; I *definitely* know I'm not like anyone else."

The waitress came up and took their orders of a Pepsi each, and Anna said, "My dad almost didn't let me come."

"He likes to keep you safe, doesn't he?"

"Yeah." She grinned. "He's the best."

"So what did he find in Romania?"

"Oh come on," Anna groaned. "Not tonight, Damien, please."

"Come on."

"Well, he found a myth about an alleged ancestor of Vlad the Impaler. Some penniless magician who came to a house of vampires and was killed in the struggle for his own life."

"What happened after that?"

"The head of the vampires made an amulet that allowed his kind to be invincible. No matter how often they were killed, they could always return if someone so much as touched the amulet. And when it was exposed to the first ray of sunlight after the full moon, they would be able to walk in daylight." She frowned. "Creepy, isn't it?"

"Did he find out if anyone's touched it lately?"

"I don't know, and I don't care to know," Anna said roughly.

"I don't know," Damien countered. "Don't you think it would be great to be able to fly and hypnotize, and go wherever you wanted to go without anyone to stop you?"

"But wouldn't you hate never being able to see the sun, or have normal friendships? Besides, the thought of living off blood is just disgusting." The waitress returned with their drinks, and Anna pulled hers towards her with a sigh. "Let's not talk about this anymore, okay?" She began to slurp the sharp cola, remembering much against her wishes the feeling of being hypnotized.

"Okay, okay," Damien conceded. "I didn't mean to offend you or anything, Anna, I was just curious."

"Hmph," she grunted between sips. "You have no idea how much I wish my dad had a normal job sometimes."

"You mean like a night salesperson at the mall?" he asked innocently.

Anna narrowed her eyes at him. "Don't be ridiculous." But she smiled all the same. He was so funny and carefree. Just how she always wished she could be. Now he walked over to the CD player. He fed it a few dollars, punched in a few keys, and Every Rose Has Its Thorn, Anna's favorite song, came out.

"Come on, Anna, dance with me," he called out. Laughing, she got up and walked over to dance with him.

"I didn't know you liked Poison."

"I've seen 'em in concert twice." Damien said. "You know what, you should come next time."

"Yeah, right! I'd have to fight World War Three with my aunt."

"But I wouldn't be alone." He put his hands on her shoulders and turned her to face him. "It's a lot less fun alone. You can't say no after I got you away from your aunt tonight."

"We'll see." Anna gave him a calculating look as she continued to dance.

"You have an excellent sense of rhythm," Damien said as he spun her out and then back. "Almost like a heartbeat. Have you ever thought about how unique a heartbeat is, Anna? It's practically the only thing keeping us alive, and we never even think about it. We never realize how delicate a balance it is, that it could suddenly just stop."

Damien could feel the girl getting weaker in his arms. Master Morugan would be very pleased that he had succeeded in giving this girl, the human who possessed the Crystal of Amadyn the clan desired so vociferously, to them all on his own.

He put one arm around her waist, his hand resting on her thigh, and brushed his lips against her slender neck. Now! There were few other patrons, and his hypnosis was taking hold of them all. He had only to bite the girl quickly-she wouldn't feel a thing-and in mere moments she would be dead, leaving a clear path to the crystal. He would prove his loyalty.

But suddenly Anna became aware of the hand at her thigh, and his lips at her neck, and she screamed in horror.

"Damien, what the hell are you doing?" She pulled his hands off her and slapped him as hard as she could, then kicked him. "I didn't give you permission to go that far with me, you know? You don't know me; you need to respect my limits." With that she kicked him once more for good measure, then she grabbed her purse, paid for her drink, and marched to the door. "I'm outta here."

The vampire remained frozen on the floor in disbelief. Not only had he failed to kill the girl, she had humiliated him. Hell, she might even have guessed that she possessed the Crystal of Amadyn, and that he had purposely sold it to her to make her a target for the clan! Never mind, it wasn't over.

"Oh, I'll get her back," he muttered furiously as he stood up. "I'll get her."

"What was that?" another girl called from across the room. It took him a moment to realize that the other patrons were coming back to themselves.

"Nothing," he said quickly, "Nothing at all," And he also departed.

Anna stormed out to the sidewalk and began the walk home; no way was she going to wait for her father. She walked onward and onward, all the way back to Central Park. Stopping to catch her breath, she realized her head was pounding, much as it had when Lysander had accidentally hypnotized her.

I'm such an idiot, she thought furiously. *I should have known he didn't mean a word of what he said.*

Just then an angry shout caught her attention. "I'm not going to tell you again, parasite, you'd better tell me where the rest of the clan is!"

To her horror, it was Lysander who shouted back, "I do not know where those horrid beasts are! What have we to do with one another?"

Anna crept around behind a stone fountain, hidden from view. The two men clashed blades again and again. The stranger, obviously a vampire hunter was pushing Lysander back towards a Marigold bush.

"Well, from the looks of things, a damn sight more than is good for you!" The hunter slashed at Lysander, just missing him.

Anna barely knew the young vampire, and yet she felt a fierce desire to help him. With an angry scream, she rounded on the Vampire hunter and pummeled him.

"Leave him alone, you son of a bitch!"

"You little pest!" The furious hunter seized Anna's wrist in an iron grip, and scalded her skin with an incantation. The girl screamed in pain as his grip tightened.

Finally, when she thought she would go mad with anguish, he thrust her aside roughly and snarled,

"That'll teach you to get in my way! Now, get out of here, before I kill you next!"

To Lysander's surprise, the girl stood but did not run.

"He is telling the truth!" she gasped; the pain was unbelievable. "Leave him alone."

"This is none of your concern, girl!" snarled the hunter furiously. "I said, get out of here!"

"No!" Anna shrieked, and she lashed out at the vampire hunter even more wildly, even more erratically. She was going to get hurt, he just knew it. "He-is-my-FRIEND!" She attempted to kick the sword from his hand, but aimed too low, and he caught her once more, searing her even worse. Her screams were deafening.

"Enough." Lysander struggled to his feet and muttered something in a language Anna didn't know. Instantly the hunter dropped to the ground, out cold.

Lysander turned his attention to the badly wounded girl, slumped against the Marigold bush, gasping for breath.

Unbelievable, he thought. *She did all that for me. Me.*

This has never happened before.

"Anna!" He knelt beside her and took her hands in his, frowning at the deep burns the hunter's incantation had left. It was plain to see that he had paralyzed the hunter not a moment too soon.

She needs help, he thought frantically. But how? Magical wounds could be healed only by magic.

Oh, don't be ridiculous! He chastised himself. After all, he had saved Kari because he had wished it. He needed merely to do the same now.

"Hold on."

Concentrating hard, the vampire began to mutter an incantation in his native language. He did not focus on his hatred of Morugan`s clan or his loathing of the hunters, but on his desire to heal the brave child.

Anna gasped as a freezing cold shot through her, but as she watched the burns began to fade. In a few moments they had healed completely.

"Relax, Anna. You're all right."

Anna took a shuddery breath as the pain receded. She relaxed her hands, which moments before had been rigid with pain.

"Th-thank you, Lysander," she finally managed to say. "Wow, I didn't know you could do that."

He grinned. "There's more to me than people think."

"How-how was he able to burn me like that?"

"It's part of being a vampire. A hunter's magic punishes not only him, but all those with whom he is affiliated. I should have told you," The vampire said morosely.

Anna grinned. "Well, that one won't be bothering you again anytime soon."

"I daresay not. Come on, I'll take you home. Your father must be frantic."

They took off into the sky.

"So what were you doing out at this hour anyway?"

"This guy I knew asked me out, and I said yes. At first he acted all sweet and attentive, but before I knew it he was pawing all over me." She frowned. "I feel so stupid."

"You weren't being foolish," Lysander admonished. "Anna, if you don't take a chance you'll never find someone who appreciates you."

"You know, I do have someone. I've been like a new person these last days. Happier. My father is pleased about it, and I know my mom would be, too."

They landed in Anna's backyard.

"Your mother," Lysander said. "You didn't mention her."

"She died a few years ago. It was the most painful thing; she was so kind and helpful to everyone, especially me." Anna stretched out on the grass.

"She was an author of children's poems, and hers were always very popular. I write poems too, I have a whole bunch of them."

"I would like to hear one."

Anna opened her purse and fished out the small notebook. She began flipping through the pages until she stopped and said, "This is a good one."

Lysander knelt beside her and she began to read:

"Some days it seems like I can't wait for the sunset
Can't wait to see the diamonds in the sky shine down
Cause when you're all alone no one can see you frown
You're tired of the way they see you
You never have the time of day
Who says its right to keep the unknown hidden away?"

Anna shut the book. "The unknown. That's us."

"That's us." Lysander grinned. "She has given you a wonderful gift, Anna."

"I've been trying to get published," Anna said, grinning back." I found a company, and they've been looking at a bunch of stuff I've sent in. So, what does a vampire who dislikes human blood find interesting?"

Lysander was speechless with wonder. No one had displayed this much interest in him for years and years, not since he had left his family.

"Well," he finally said, a bit hesitantly. "I- I used to collect different herbs, but I haven't had the heart for it in a very long time."

"Herbs? Like what?"

"Close your eyes." She closed her eyes. He plucked a sprig of fresh mint from the ground and held it up to her nose so she could catch its mild, sweet scent. "Breathe deeply," he instructed.

She inhaled deeply. "Smells good. Like peppermint."

"Very good." He grinned.

"I didn't know we even had wild mint here."

"You can find a lot of hidden things when you know where to look for them," Lysander said, grinning. "Years ago doctors used this to treat fevers, and it generally worked very well."

"What else do you collect?"

"Well, there are lots." He took out a fresh branch whose red and gold leaves were as familiar to him as his native soil, and placed it in her hand. "This one is called Tamarind."

"Pretty," she said, turning the branch around in her hand.

"Well, it's a bit more than just a pleasant plant," he said grinning. "This one was used to combat Hypothermia."

"You mean what happened when people were out in the cold too long and got sick?"

"That's right."

"That's interesting," Anna said, and he could see that she was speaking in earnest. "You know, I've never liked how superficial this town feels, with its sidewalks and things. I can see why you would like Central Park. That place brought me a lot of comfort when I lost my mom."

"It's a beautiful place, isn't it?"

She nodded. "I would come there when I wanted to be alone. But I never thought I would find someone like you there. Or that lunatic." She narrowed her eyes. "I know it was stupid of me to try to fight him off, but he just made me so angry."

"It was brave. You showed that you trust me, and that's not something anyone can do. Anna, you could have been killed."

She grinned. "I'm not sorry I did it, either."

Over the next few weeks the two spent many hours together, talking late into the night. He taught her about all the medicinal plants he knew of, and their functions in healing, and she, in turn, shared her poems with him, something she would have never thought of doing with anyone except her mother. It was a wonderful feeling, finally experiencing true friendship again after he had been alone for so long.

"These are interesting," Anna said one night, plucking some pretty green plants with little yellow blossoms. "I don't think I've ever seen these before. What are they called?"

Lysander looked at them carefully. "That is called Wormwood. It was generally used as an anesthetic, mostly along with other herbs to induce a deep sleep."

"Like when someone was having surgery done, or when they were in a lot of pain, right?"

"Yes, that's right."

"How do you know so much about herbs and medicines and things like that?"

"My family raised crops for a living, so I grew up with a familiarity of the land. Our way of life was very humble, and I wanted to do more for them, so when I got older I went to the university and started studying medicine, then a few years into it I found work at a clinic in town. I supplemented their income with my earnings whenever I could."

"That was generous of you," Anna said.

He chuckled. "Actually my father considered it base treachery at first. My sister Arania made him change his mind, though, eventually. She used to go along with me to collect herbs in the forest, and a great help she was too." He was glad to be remembering his sister in a pleasant way, not just how she had been at the time of her death. "She was a remarkable person. I don't think I've ever met someone who suffered more than she did, but she was always putting herself second to me and to our parents."

"You have a sister?"

"I did," Lysander said, and there was sadness in the young vampire's voice. "I lost her to Typhoid many years ago, nothing I did made any difference. She made me promise that I would use my skills to help people wherever I went, which is a vow that has proven very difficult to make good on. You see, it was soon after that, very soon after, that I became what I am now."

"That's terrible," Anna breathed, filled with empathy for her strange friend. "It sounds like you really loved her a lot."

"I still do," Lysander said wistfully. "More than anything, my parents, too. My biggest regret was that I was never able to see them again." After a moments silence, he asked, "Anna, I've been wondering, what happened to your mother? That is, if you don't mind me asking," he added hastily.

"Lukemia," Anna said, finding to her great surprise that she didn't mind Lysander asking about her mother in the least. "She fought it as hard as she could, but it took her so fast we barely had time to blink. There are still some illnesses today that can't be cured."

"I-I am very sorry to hear that."

"I didn't think my father would ever get over it. He still keeps a tight watch on me, you know, even though he isn't around much."

"He cares about you."

"I know. I just wish my dad would let me go with him sometimes instead of having me stay with my aunt all the time."

"You don't get on?"

Anna frowned. "Dad had me move in with her because he wanted me to have a stable home, but she's a dragon. All we do is argue." After a moment she said, "My dad told me a few days ago about a gemstone that can turn vampires back. Would you use it, Lysander? You could be with your family again if you went back to how you were before. They must miss you terribly."

Lysander thought about this, about what it would be like to walk about in daylight again, to see his parents and his little sister. To see the beautiful fields he had left behind in Bucharest all those years ago. He could not deny it; he ached for a way to make it happen.

"No," he finally said. "I couldn't. They would be long gone by now. It does not do to dwell on the past and forget to live for the present." He knelt in the grass, his eyes on the ground. "However you might like to."

"I'm sorry," Anna said. "I didn't mean to...I-I know I'm not Arania." She sat beside him tentatively, afraid that she had made him angry, but when he raised his head to look at her, he was smiling.

"There's nothing wrong with a new reason to hope for better times." He put an arm around her. "Come here." She grinned, hugging back. He could barely remember when he had last embraced someone, and it felt so wonderful that he might have gladly stayed there with her for eternity.

How foolish he had been to ever distance himself from people like her, he thought.

After a minute Anna said, "I've made a new poem, it's about a friend of mine, a very special one."

"Is it?" He looked over her shoulder as she opened the book and rifled through the pages.

"Here it is." She began to read:

> *I know what it's like to be alone*
> *Feeling the rain sting my eyes as I walk*
> *I never thought I would feel the warmth of a fire*
> *Watching my name make everyone around me balk*
> *Now you hold me in your arms*
> *And I know I will always be safe*
> *So let lightning split the sky in two*
> *Tomorrow will be a brighter day."*

"It's wonderful, Anna." Lysander was beaming.

"Glad you like it, I had a feeling you would." She smiled back at him. "I just hope I never see a day when lightning splits the sky in two, that would be way scarier than any vampire."

"I agree."

"Well, at least if that happened we wouldn't be alone when it did." Anna closed the book and placed it back into her purse. "I think a good friend is kind of like an umbrella on a rainy day. They protect you, like an umbrella protects you from the rain. Too bad they're so hard to find, though."

"I know how that feels," he said, looking into those green eyes that seemed to glow in the dark. "I`ve been alone for a long time, and I almost forgot at one point what being a friend is like."

"You won't forget," Anna replied, grinning mischievously. "I won't let you."

He laughed. "All right."

Anna looked up at the star studded sky, feeling more at ease with Lysander at her side than, possibly, she had ever felt before. But something was nagging at her from the inside. He did not behave at all like a vampire, and she was curious-needed to know-how it had come about. But how could she ask such a thing?

"Lysander?"

"Hmm?"

"I've been wondering-how exactly did it happen?"

He did not need to ask what it was that she was referring to.

"I was just curious. I mean," She added precariously, her face reddening, "you don't have to answer if you don't want to. I know it's not something you like to think about."

Lysander did not reply at once, but merely looked down at her as he stroked her long, blond hair-it was smooth as cornsilk. She looked over her shoulder at him, her expression a mixture of terrorized anticipation and regret. Finally, after a sizeable silence, he spoke.

"The simple truth of it, Anna, is that I was a coward. That was what began the whole thing."

She frowned quizzically. "I don't understand."

"It began with my sister," he explained. "I refused to believe that she was dying, even though she knew it herself. After she was gone, I went wild with grief."

"Well, that's understandable."

He shook his head. "You don't understand. I ran away from home. I abandoned my parents and ran off into the forest, wishing that I, too, would depart this life so I could be with her once more. My family lived in Bucharest, Romania, and it was the middle of winter. A lot of people died during that time of year because it's very cold in Romania during the winter months and there were very few doctors in Bucharest. It was a very poor town."

Anna said nothing, but kept her eyes on him, never blinking.

"I walked a very long way," Lysander continued, his voice low. "It seemed to me that anything would be better than to stay in that town. It was cowardly of me, I know. Like I said, there are few doctors in Bucharest, and I, who had been trained by one of the best there was, left them to the mercy of that terrible time. I surely had as much of an obligation to stay at the hospital as any good physician."

"That's ridiculous," Anna reprimanded him. "You saved my life when that lunatic burned me."

"I know that now. But I never got the chance to reconsider my decision. You see, that very night, while I was gathering firewood, I heard footsteps behind me. I fled deeper and deeper into the forest, but the footsteps followed. I heard laughter, the most terrible laughter, in my ears. And finally, when I was breathless with fatigue, I felt a terrible pain at my neck that became stronger as the moments passed. I could feel myself getting weaker all the while; I was losing a lot of blood."

"The vampire," Anna murmured.

"Yes. I collapsed in a faint, and when I woke up I could feel that I was different. I could hear things that were impossible for me to hear before. I could smell things that had been hidden to me, most particularly the blood of humans. It attracted me, and yet the idea of killing repulsed me more than the scent of their blood attracted me. I vowed from then on that I would never kill a human being, never taint another as I had been tainted. So I lived in isolation, away from everyone. Year in and year out, since that winter in 1875."

"One hundred and twenty years," Anna murmured.

"That's right."

"And you,. You've never......?"

"Bitten anyone?" He smiled grimly. "Never."

"What did you live off of, then?"

"Whatever was available where I happened to be at the time. I moved a lot, you see, I felt it was best to not stay in any one place long. Big cities like this were the most difficult, most of the time I had to make do with rats."

Anna made a face. "That's disgusting."

Lysander smiled, for real this time. "Beggars can't be choosers, my dear."

"No, I suppose not."

Just then a familiar blue Pontiac pulled into the driveway. Lysander gave an angry hiss as the bright high beams stung his eyes.

"Oh, no," Anna muttered.

Mr. Harper climbed out. "Anna, it's after ten. What are you doing out here?"

"I'm sorry, Dad."

"You needn't be alarmed, sir," Lysander said. "We're hardly strangers. Anna is quite safe with me."

Mr. Harper's brown eyes went wide as silver dollars as he took in the strange man standing beside his daughter. "Who are you?"

"He's my friend," Anna cut in sharply.

"Anna, do you know what he *is?*" Mr. Harper had studied vampire folklore for years, yes, but it had never crossed is mind that they might actually be real, or that he might meet one. It was not an overstatement to say that he was terrified.

"You know?" Anna asked, shocked.

"I saw his eyes flash red when I pulled up." Mr. Harper frowned.

"Yes, he's a vampire. *And* he's my friend."

"Oh, really." Mr. Harper glared at the intruder, his fear quickly giving way to anger and contempt. "It seems like a foolish reason to be out walking around in plain view of hunters."

These words stung, but Lysander was not about to be insulted by a mortal man, a feeble specimen by all accounts, who, for all his bluster, was easy prey.

"You will find, Sir," he said curtly, "that all vampires are *not* created equal. And you would do well to remember this before you snub those who would help you in these dangerous times." He turned from him stiffly. "Good evening to you." And with that he took flight.

"Lysander," Anna said sadly, watching him go.

"Anna, come inside," Mr. Harper called.

Anna glared at him. "Dad! How could you?" Then she ran into the house, ran up to her room, and when she had closed the door, sank to the floor in despair. *I'll never see him again,* she thought as she wept bitterly.

V

Dangers Untold,
Hardships Without Number

Lysander flew high above the city, his mind whirring at top speed. Morugan would be expecting him back soon, and the Head Vampire had made it clear that he would not tolerate anyone who returned empty-handed. But Lysander knew he must proceed with his plan if his friend were to survive.

Suddenly the answer came to him; magic! The original had been created out of nothing, so what was to stop him from creating a duplicate in the same way? After all, he was a descendent of Amadyn, was he not?

Lysander flew to Central Park and landed in the soft dirt. He closed his eyes and pictured the crystal, sun-yellow, about the size of a strawberry, set in silver filigree. He pictured the way it glittered in the moonlight, imagined the weight of it in his hand, saw the delicate chain from which it hung.

In a flash of moonlight the duplicate materialized. Lysander turned it around in his hand; it was perfect! Absolutely flawless! "Oh, you will have your crystal, Morugan," he said, snickering. "Be assured of that!" Then he took flight for Bluerock Manor.

"Lysander, where have you been?" Morugan demanded when the youth landed on the grounds of Bluerock Manor. "The night wanes. Have you done what I bade you?"

"Yes, Uncle. The crystal of Amadyn is indeed in this city. You were right all along."

"Of course I was right." Morugan grinned his fanged grin. "Where did you find it? Who had it?"

"I did not see anyone with the crystal, they must have discarded it. I found it in Central Park, buried under the ground. I could feel it pulsing. Unfortunately I could not unearth it, humans were approaching."

"That is quite all right. We will unearth it now. Lead on, Lad, lead on!"

And that is exactly what Lysander did. Twenty minutes later Morugan pulled Lysander's creation out from the dirt as the clan watched.

"Yes, oh yes, we will triumph, brothers." He cackled as he held it aloft. "I declare it, not one human will be left alive when we are through."

"Anna, what is wrong with you?" Jennifer demanded at school the next day. "It's been three weeks, and you haven't said anything about Damien, I thought you'd be bragging like crazy."

Anna sighed. "There's nothing to brag about. There's nothing to *talk* about. The guy was a creep, plain and simple."

"What do you mean? What'd he do?"

"Jen, he pawed me over like I was a piece of meat or something. It was disgusting."

"Ew. Sorry, Anna. But you can't let one bad experience sour you. There are plenty of other fish in the sea."

"Yeah, well, after what happened Saturday I don't think I'll be fishing again anytime real soon," Anna said disdainfully. "You know what, when he was holding me while we danced my mind went completely blank. I couldn't remember where I was or anything. And when I came out of it I had such a migraine I could barely think."

"Weird," Jennifer mumbled. Anna nodded. "I think we should do something boy-free. There's a really good movie at the multiplex. Do you think your dad will let you go alone tonight?"

"Maybe." Anna still couldn't forget the cold way her father had acted towards Lysander, even though he really was very kind. She wouldn't have blamed her father if he never let her go out again.

"It'll be fine, Anna," Jennifer said. "You just need to chill out and forget all this for awhile."

"Sounds cool. I'll ask him."

"What are you working on?" Mr. Harper asked later that evening.

Anna looked up from the textbook she had been reading. "History. I'm almost done." She frowned as she erased a sentence she had written on the timeline she was to complete for the next day.

Mr. Harper chuckled. "Not very happy about it, are you?"

"Not really. It's about the Holocaust." She etched out a few more sentences, and then shut the book. "Dad, I need to talk to you."

"About what?"

"About what happened last night. I know you must have been frightened."

Her father sighed. "Frightened? Anna, I-I've never been more terrified. I keep thinking he'll come in the night and attack you."

"If he wanted to do that, I think he would have done it already."

"Don't be too sure," he said. "It's in a vampire's nature to beguile their prey before they attack. They are masters of deception."

"You think Lysander is leading me on?"

"Is that his name?"

"Yes. And for the record, he's already hypnotized me once."

"He has?" Mr. Harper asked, his eyes going wide.

"Yes. Before you got here. Dad, I thought I was dead. But he revived me and watched over me. I trust him."

"I just don't want anything to happen to you," Mr. Harper said sadly. "You're all I have to live for, Anna. You know that, don't you?" He hugged her.

"Yes," Anna laughed. "Everything is going to be fine, Dad. So, Jennifer asked me out to the movies tonight. We'll be back by eight."

"Have you finished all your homework?"

"Yes."

"You're definitely going to be back by eight?"

"Definitely."

"Go have some fun," Her father said.

Anna enjoyed the movie and, and went home feeling happier than she would have thought possible. *Thank God for Jennifer,* she thought as she said goodbye. Even though she still felt bad about what had happened between Lysander and her father, she knew she could handle living in New York so long as she had one friend.

"Anna, I just got a call from one of my assistants," Her father said when she entered the house. "I'll have to leave earlier than I thought. We're going to Moscow."

"You'll have to give me the address so I can write to you," Anna said, smiling sadly. "I want to know everything that happens."

"I promise I'll tell you everything. Actually I thought you'd be asking to come along. You never seemed very happy here."

"It's not too bad. It took some getting used to, like everything else. But I'm perfectly fine with staying." Anna smiled for real now. "Maybe we can get together when school lets out this summer."

"Sure, honey. Now I think it's time for you to go to bed, you have that test in Algebra tomorrow."

"Good night." Anna went up to her room.

Sometime later Lysander entered the room. He knelt at his friend's side, and it broke his heart to think that, sometime soon, he would have to leave her for good.

How peaceful she looked in her slumber! Would he never be able to rest as profoundly as this little mortal?

"Forgive me, Anna." He sighed. "It is a wretch that we should be separated."

Just then Anna roused. "Lysander." She got quickly to her feet. "I thought I'd never see you again. Sorry about Dad."

"That's all right. He was frightened and wanted to protect you." He drew a breath; better to get it over with right away. "Listen, Anna- it would be best if we didn't meet anymore."

A confused expression came over Anna's face. "What? Why?"

"This is why." He pulled out the yellow gemstone from where it had been stashed. "This is the gemstone you mentioned before. You know what it can do. Morugan is after it, and also after us."

"Who is Morugan?"

"The head of the clan I belong to."

"*Clan?*" Anna squeaked, terrified. "Exactly how many of you are there?"

"A few, and there are more elsewhere. They are looking to him to lead the purge of mortals and establish a new regime."

"He wants us all dead?" Anna asked, shivering with fright.

Lysander looked out the window, as though he was worried they might be overheard.

"He is a demon of a creature, Anna," he said severely. "Many centuries ago Morugan was a human, just like me. He was a soldier in the Romanian army, and very well respected. However, one year after the end of a war overseas, the war crimes tribunal sentenced him to a decade of isolation in the mountains for committing war crimes against the enemy. They proclaimed that he had abused and killed many families in order to plunder their strongboxes. It was untrue, however. In fact, the reason they convicted him was that the enemy was bribing the war crimes tribunal with ten thousand pieces of silver-a lot of money in that time."

"Didn't anyone know that it wasn't true?"

Lysander shook his head. "No one dared to protest the word of the war crimes tribunal. It was a branch of the highest court in the land, and the penalty was death. Everyone was terrified out of their wits, they didn't know what to do."

"Cowards," she said angrily.

"And that's not even the worst of it." Lysander sighed as though continuing in his story would cost him all his grit. "When Morugan returned to his village, he discovered that his family was gone, wife and children all. They had been put to death on the gallows. It's been said that the only things of theirs he ever recovered were one small portrait of his family, and a gemstone that had passed down from one generation to the next. This gemstone, in fact." He tapped the faceted surface of the stone with one finger, and it gave a flash of yellow light.

"That's terrible," Anna gasped. She had never felt so horrified in her life.

"Morugan went mad with grief for his family," Lysander continued. "He became consumed by the need for revenge, sneaking into houses and murdering whole families in the dead of night. This went on for a good ten years, until finally his actions caught up with him. The church was called in: they exorcized him for many hours until he was worse than dead."

"What do you mean?" Anna kept her eyes locked on his, waiting for him to answer. Something told her she did not want him to answer, but that she needed to know.

Lysander looked at her with a pained expression: clearly he did not want to give the answer any more than she wanted to hear it.

"Well, an exorcism is meant to destroy the corrupt soul and leave the body intact. But in Morugan's case, it worked in the opposite way. The priest's spell left Morugan's soul very much alive while his body was destroyed, so the evil that had taken root inside him was never truly killed. It flitted around until it took up residence in a cannibalistic corpse resurrected from the dead by the family heirloom that was known as Amadyn's amulet, named after the sorcerer Morugan's ancestor had slain centuries before."

Anna gasped in fright.

"From then on he was truly a monster. His bloodlust had only grown since his rebirth, and every time he was banished by a holyman, he was able to return thanks to Amadyn's amulet. He started using it as a way to lead himself to new victims, leaving it where some unwitting mortal would come across it. One touch was all it took to bring the vampires to that person's exact location, and in order to keep their secret, the summoner would be drained of their blood instantly."

Anna sat frozen on the edge of her bed, not able to move, barely able to breathe. What a frightening tale!

"Morugan has done this more times than can be counted in the ensuing years," Lysander said, both melancholy and angry at himself for frightening Anna. "When I realized what that gemstone was, I attempted to destroy it. Morugan has never accused me, but I get the fleeting impression that he knows more than he is letting on." He sighed. "I have seen him terrorize whole cities, and with the war going on with the vampire hunters, it would be a very accurate assumption to say he might well be more dangerous now than ever before."

"Me," Anna muttered. "He wants me. I'm the one who summoned the vampires."

"I am afraid so. I have temporarily deterred them, but the duplicate will not buy us much time." He frowned. "I cannot allow an innocent to suffer for their greed."

"You tricked them? Just to keep me safe?" Anna's green eyes widened to the size of saucers. "Lysander-how can I ever thank you?"

"Get rid of this evil thing, Anna, Quickly. Stay near to your father, for he would give up his life rather than see you come to harm. Beware of anyone who tries to beguile you, and above all, never venture out at night alone. Neither side would think twice about killing a young girl who got in the middle of their fighting."

Anna nodded, and then asked, "But what about you? You can't fight them alone, they'll kill you."

"I must. There are worse things than death."

Anna sank weakly into her desk chair and brushed her blond waves out of her face, trying to master herself. She could not believe what she was hearing, could not believe her amazing new friend was going to give himself up as a sacrificial lamb, just when they were really beginning to get to know one another.

"Anna-Anna, look at me."

She looked at him; he was walking over to her.

"I knew from the moment I first laid eyes on you that you were worth protecting." He took her chin in his hand and gently raised her head up so he could see her face, brushing away the tears on her cheek with his thumb. "You have brought me more joy than you could ever know, my darling, and I would gladly give up my life for yours."

Anna felt tears pricking at her eyes again. She had known, in her heart of hearts that this moment must come eventually, but the pain of it now that it was time overwhelmed her. "You're a great friend, Lysander," she said in a constricted voice.

"Stay strong, Anna," he said as he put his arms around her and they hugged for the last time. "I will always love you, remember that." Then, in a flash, he was gone.

"Goodbye," Anna said softly. She grasped the crystal so tightly that it hurt, and tears sprang into her eyes.

As soon as Lysander had left a figure shrouded in darkness, hidden in the trees, let out a soft cackle.

"Very clever of you, Lysander, you freak," he said. "Feed the most powerful vampire on earth a pack of well-composed lies. But you did not foresee me in your clever little plan, did you?" He rose up and looked into Anna Harper's window. She sat on her bed, a frown on her pretty face.

"I know your secrets. Oh yes, I know them all! And so will the Master, in due course. Oh, you are a fool,

Lysander Heistad, a fool!" He whizzed off into the night, laughing like mad.

Late that night Morugan walked out to the highest window in Bluerock Manor and faced a waxing golden moon.

"It is time." Suddenly he let out a howl, a long, loud, mournful sound that reverberated off the stone walls.

"Really, Uncle," Lysander objected "Must you make such a racket?"

But Morugan refused to desist. He merely howled louder and louder until his pet timber wolf rose from his basket and added his own snarls and grunts to the din. He persisted until a cavalry of dark shapes could be seen silhouetted against the moon, growing larger and larger.

"Welcome, brothers!" he called out at last. "Do come in, the journey has no doubt tired you."

"I certainly hope you have called us for some very important news, Morugan," an old man said, handing his cloak to Lysander. "Every year it becomes more taxing." Two women, each a bit older than Lysander himself, did the same, as well as an older woman and another man.

"Don't drag them on the floor, boy," he barked at Lysander. "They were expensive."

"Well, don't just stand there. Show our guests to the ballroom." Morugan glared unpleasantly at his nephew, who struggled with the load. Lysander made his way unsteadily down the staircase and through the corridors towards the ballroom. Quiet mutterings flew thickly behind him.

"What a strange boy."

"Never liked him."

Finally he pushed open the shining oak doors and the guests filed in, seating themselves at the long tables. Morugan stood at the front of the room and smiled his fanged smile.

"Be seated, everyone. We have much to discuss." Then his gaze drifted to is nephew at the back of the room, and his smile vanished. "Wine, Lysander, where are your manners?"

Suppressing a sigh, Lysander left the room as Morugan began to talk of the drudges of city life, the lights at night, the constant noises, and the difficulty in procuring sustenance. He riffled through the wine selection, choosing three bottles of Merlot and three of Chardonnay. He located the appropriate glasses and made his way silently back to the ballroom. However, just as he was about to open the doors, Vlad bounded over to him and nipped at his ankles.

"Vlad, go away," Lysander groaned. He kicked at the wolf, but Vlad only growled and tugged harder.

"Leave me!" In the melee Lysander lost his balance, and one of the glasses fell from the tray and crashed to pieces on the floor.

"What the devil is going on out there?" Morugan demanded irritably.

"Nothing. It's nothing." The youth quickly cleared away the glass and entered the ballroom, placing the tray on the back table.

"Friends," Morugan proclaimed, "I have called you here tonight because I have some most interesting news." Immediate silence fell over the room as all turned to face the Head Vampire. "As you all know, well over two thousand years ago, the sorcerer Amadyn lost his dear wife Mariela in childbirth and went off into the forest alone to grieve, not stopping for near to a fortnight. Whilst roaming he happened upon the castle of our descendant, Heirchan. The two began a fierce battle and, for all his skill, Amadyn was left dead on the floor. As a celebration of his victory, Heirchan created this amulet. It would allow him to be resurrected again and again, no matter how many times he was defeated in a fight, so that he was never truly conquerable. Several years later he was killed by a vampire hunter, who destroyed the crystal. As you know, it was I who repaired the gemstone, and thus carried on the tradition begun by our lord, as it was my birthright as his direct descendant. However, we have yet to harness the second part of the crystal's power, the ability to make us invincible to not only physical wounds, but to sunlight as well. I have dreamt of it for centuries, and so, I trust, have you."

The listeners roared their approval. Lysander felt revulsion fill him, but he bit back his retort; he knew he must not provoke their wrath until exactly the opportune time or his friend would be doomed as well. He must protect her at all costs.

"Yes, yes," Morugan called commandingly. "Well, the crystal was lost over a century ago, by means of which we have never discovered. But no longer. You are all clever, swift hunters, my friends, and together the world stands not a chance against us when we can rule the day as we rule the night. It gives me great pleasure to announce to you tonight that the Crystal of Amadyn is at last ours once again." He held Lysander's creation aloft for everyone to see.

"How has this come to be?" asked a woman near the back of the room.

"Ah, I am glad to hear you ask." Morugan smiled once more, a wider and more frightening smile than Lysander had ever seen. "I must admit I was taken quite aback when I heard the news myself. However,

I am grateful indeed for the help of my dear nephew Lysander."

Every head in the room turned to face the young vampire. Lysander did not trust himself to speak; he stood perfectly still as snatches of conversation reached him.

"Is it possible?"

"Him?"

"I say!"

"Yes," Morugan called over the din. "It was Lysander who located the gem, who secured this victory for us. Well done, boy, well done."

Applause began, slowly at first, then louder and louder.

Suddenly an unfamiliar voice called out over the ruckus, "Why are you praising *him*? *He* is not loyal to the clan, nor has he done a thing for us."

There was instant silence. Lysander's eyes darted around in search of the speaker.

"Who said that?" Morugan demanded. He looked around, his eyes wide, alarmed.

"I did." A young vampire, no older than Lysander himself, strode into the light. He had shaggy yellow hair and pale skin, and his handsome face was contorted in a cruel sneer.

"And who might you be, my lad?" Morugan asked, swiftly reclaiming his composure.

The newcomer strode to the front of the room stopping just in front of the Head Vampire. "My name is Darvis Kymbal. For many moon cycles now I have sought to be welcomed into your clan. I have been following this nephew of yours and I am here tonight to expose him for what he is; a fraud! Master Morugan, the crystal you hold in your hand is not the true Crystal of Amadyn but a cleverly devised duplicate meant to deter you."

Morugan looked from the crystal he held in his hand, to his nephew, to the newcomer, and then back to the crystal. "You-you are quite sure?"

"Absolutely certain. I saw him forge it with my own eyes."

"Lysander!!!" Morugan`s howl of rage was enough to raise the dead.

"And this is but the latest of his transgressions." Kymbal`s blue eyes glittered like sapphires as he continued eagerly. "You see, it was *I* who located the true crystal, several moon cycles ago, in an abandoned mineshaft outside the city. Knowing you and your clan desired to possess it, I decided to plant it on a mortal being to make them a target for you. I adopted the guise of a night salesman and began my search for the one I would use. Barely more than a fortnight ago, I decided on one girl, Anna Harper. She was perfect for my plan, sweet, lonely, and vulnerable. And sure enough, she summoned the clan. Lysander here befriended the girl and has until now succeeded in keeping her safe." Here Kymbal broke off snickering. "But, as we have learned from Amadyn himself, there is no more potent way to doom oneself than to become entangled with mortals."

"Bring him here*! Now*!"

Several vampires seized Lysander and shoved him roughly through the crowd. Try though he might, the youth could not break their grasp. Finally they shoved him down roughly before his pacing, seething uncle.

"I knew from the very beginning that you were peculiar," Morugan began in dangerous tones, "Careless. Ignorant of our way of life. But I never for a second thought that you might be a traitor. You know the penalty for treason, Lysander." He turned to his followers. "Take him out to the fields. He will burn to a cinder at daybreak."

The assembled followers cheered in agreement.

Suddenly a voice cried out above all the others, "Oh no, you don't. I've gone through Hell and High water because of that freak. If anyone's going to kill him, it'll be me." The assembled masses turned to see a large group of vampire hunters, headed by the same weathered man that had burned Anna. Lysander hissed angrily at the sight of him.

Morugan gave a hiss of warning. "I told you, Garrison, to never disturb my followers!"

Nevertheless, Hunters surrounded the assembly of vampires, outnumbering them five to one. Where had Garrison found so many minions?

The poacher brought out a silver dagger and held it against Morugan's neck. The Head Vampire looked around and saw that his minions were similarly accosted.

"I really don't think you're in any position to argue with us, *Master*," Garrison hissed threateningly. "You see, in case you haven't noticed, we outnumber you."

"I will turn your bones to ashes!" the enraged vampire snarled, at which point Garrison brought the knife closer to his white skin.

"Now you listen to me, you revolting bastard. You know perfectly well that we're more than a match for you. You can either let us have the boy without any trouble, or it'll be your bones that burn to ashes. Don't forget, we've got magic of our own."

He held up the red crystal. "You bloodsuckers only got a taste of what this thing can do. You lucked out last time. We've sealed the doors. So make your decision."

"Ech! Do your worst! I will not comply with you, Garrison!"

"Very well." Garrison raised the crystal high.

Kymbal had broken free of his captors. Striding purposefully up to his assaulted master, he said, "No, no, no. We will gladly hand over the traitorous fraud to you. We merely ask that you do us one small favor in return."

"Really," Garrison sneered. "And what might that be?"

"There is someone whom we would like very much indeed to see here at the Manor. A girl named Anna Harper. I trust you may have met?"

Garrison looked over at Lysander and a look of recognition came over his face. "Oh, yeah. That little brat who got in my way last time I tried to kill the boy." His steely eyes bored into Lysander's. "I really would have enjoyed seeing her burn to a crisp, too."

"I offer to spare you the arduous task of killing her. We merely wish to know how to get into contact with her so we might bring her here."

"You wouldn't need help with that," Lysander shouted. "You've already tried to kill her."

The slightest twinge of color appeared in Kymbal`s pallid face. How did the traitor know this? He felt all eyes shift to him.

"It is true, I admit it. Unfortunately, she broke free of the trance I placed upon her, and she is now most distrustful of me."

"You will not succeed."

"That is where you are wrong." Kymbal`s eyes were suddenly sharp and hard as he glared at Lysander. "Her compassionate nature is her weakness. Whatever you may have told her, she will listen to her heart. She will forgive Damien Roberson for his slight in time. I need only play my role carefully." He turned to Garrison. "So, what say you? Will you tell us what we need to know?"

"Do I get the boy?"

"Yes."

"Try the phone book. There's only one Harper in Manhattan. It'll be easy."

"Phone book?" Morugan inquired.

"A technological device used in the outside world. Leave it to me, Master, I will do it."

"Very well. Get this disgraceful waste of flesh out of my sight."

Then Morugan turned his back on his nephew as the hunters pulled him to his feet, tied his wrists behind him, and led him away. He did not acknowledge his nephew's shouts in any way, did not move an inch.

The vampire hunters led Lysander down out to the van where they had parked.

"Come on, move it." Garrison shoved him hard, sending him sprawling to the ground. He could not move an inch, but the pain was nothing compared to his seething anger.

"Go near my friend," he hissed fiercely in Romanian, "And I will hunt you to the grave myself, Garrison. That is a promise."

"Wow, some threat," jeered another hunter. "How do you intend to do that when you can't even fly?"

"That's what emotions do to you." Another hunter seized Lysander by the ear and pulled him to his feet. "They make you weak, vulnerable. Whoever heard of a vampire falling for a human anyway? I thought you freaks were as weird as you could possibly get."

Lysander snarled in Romanian. "Damn you all!"

"Such language," said Kymbal`s voice. "Don't be so gloomy, Lysander. At least you will be spared hearing her scream." Lysander looked up. The other vampire was hovering above them, clearly enjoying the proceedings. The cruel smile on his face stretched from ear to ear.

"Kymbal." Lysander spat the name as though it tasted like arsenic.

"Oh, that's right. You already have heard her scream, haven't you?" Kymbal sneered wider. "I imagine that it chilled you inside, didn't it? Made you cringe, as though you could feel her pain. Made you feel like the ridiculous sentimental pushover you are."

Lysander swore in his native language again.

"Oh look, I've touched a nerve. How inconsiderate of me."

"You must not go through with this!" Lysander shouted as his captors shoved him into the van. "She is but an innocent child! Do what you will with me, but she does not deserve my punishment."

"And deny ourselves that precious blood? We would be mad to suggest it," Kymbal retorted. The door was padlocked, and he veered closer, peering right into the other vampire's eyes. Speaking in just above a whisper, he added, "You know, I almost admire the way you have been looking after Anna. Too bad she will never thank you for being a failure as a friend. I'll tell her goodbye for you, Lysander."

Lysander's dark eyes flashed angrily. "Mark my words, Kymbal, you will writhe in hell for this!"

"I've already been there. And I look forward to returning." With a cold, mocking smile Kymbal left, and the others followed.

Lysander sighed. That menace had been there the whole time! Had heard everything! How could he possibly have failed to notice? "Anna," He said in a desolate whisper.

That night the clan turned loose to terrorize the city like they never had before. At the end of two hours 350 people lay dead, far outstripping the clan's previous accomplishments.

"You have done very well, Darvis," said the Head Vampire as they prepared to take off once more.

"Think nothing of it, Master. It is an honor and a pleasure to be of service."

"I believe we have had our fill for tonight. Let us retire."

Just then Kymbal saw a light flick on at the house across the street, and a familiar redheaded figure answered the phone.

"Actually, if it pleases you, my lord, I would like to make one more stop."

"Very well," Morugan agreed. "One more."

"Hello?" Jennifer yawned into the phone.

"Jen!" came the anxious voice from the other end. "I've got something really important to tell you!" Anna had not been able to sleep, had not even thought about it.

Jennifer glanced at her clock-radio. "Anna, it's past midnight. Can't this wait until school tomorrow?"

"No. Jen, that crystal I bought from Giridali`s summoned a whole fleet of vampires. They're planning to kill everyone in town."

Jennifer sighed impatiently. Her friend was a logical person, she couldn't believe she was hearing this. "Anna, there are two problems with your theory. First of all, there are no such things as vampires."

"Yes, there are!" Anna exclaimed. "My dad has seen them, too! You can even ask him!"

"And secondly," Jennifer continued as though she had not heard, "Even if there were, it would be physically impossible for them to kill everyone in New York City. Ten million people live here, remember?"

"You've never seen one, have you?" Anna challenged. "Do you have any idea how fast they can move?"

"No," her friend said impatiently, "Because they don't exist!"

"I'm telling you, they exist, and I've seen them! Please believe me, Jen. I've never lied before, why would I make this up? Please be careful, they could be anywhere."

Jennifer groaned. "Anna, you have completely lost it. Go back to bed and call me when you're decent." Then she hung up and shut off the lights.

A few minutes later, Kymbal entered the room. "Such beauty," he said placidly, and he raised her head up. "Such purity. It is a pity that you had to find out, Jennifer." Then he bent over her and sank his fangs into her skin.

The next day at school, Anna didn't even make a pretense of listening to the teacher. She was too upset about her argument with Jennifer, and too nervous about the fact that her friend, who never missed a day of school, was not there.

"Anna!" Mr. Angler's irritating voice sliced into her thoughts like a knife. "Will you please pay attention?"

"Sorry," Anna mumbled, not feeling sorry in the least.

But when the test was passed out, Anna remained motionless while the other students began working. She hoped Jennifer was okay, even though it hurt that her friend hadn't believed her. Absentmindedly, she took the crystal out of her pocket and gazed into its faceted depths.

Lysander told me to destroy this, she thought. *But how? It's magical. I can't destroy a magical gemstone.*

Just then Mr. Angler shouted, "Anna Harper! What are you doing?"

He was glaring at her looking absolutely furious.

"Nothing." She quickly stashed the gem out of sight.

"Yes, exactly. Nothing. And I am tired of it! If you will not do your work, then go to the principal's office. Now!"

Several students snickered as Anna made her way out of the classroom, but she was too angry to say a word.

"Fine," she spat once she was alone in the corridors. "I can think of a million things more important than that stupid test anyway." She was about to knock on the door of the principal's office when an announcement came on over the Intercom system.

"Attention, everyone. This afternoon I received word that we have lost one of our students. Jennifer Mendez, a freshman, was found dead along with her parents this morning. The cause for their deaths is, at present, unknown, although the police suspect that they may have been attacked by wolves. Jennifer was an excellent student and a friend to many here at Rockefeller High, and I now ask that we all observe a moment of silence."

Anna sank weakly to the floor, tears streaming down her face. She knew what had happened to Jennifer's family, and wolves had nothing to do with it. They had been attacked by vampires; she knew it as certainly as though she had seen it for herself. Lysander was right.

Suddenly the door opened, and the principal walked out. "Anna! Why aren't you in class?" She helped the girl to her feet.

"She was my best friend," Anna croaked. "She was my best friend, and I'll never see her again."

"Jennifer was?" The girl nodded dumbly. "I think you should go home for the rest of the day. Is there someone who can come and pick you up?"

"My dad," Anna said in a weak voice. She told the principal her phone number, and her father came for her ten minutes later.

"Oh, Anna, I am so sorry," he said, hugging her. All she could think about was, soon she would be completely alone. How could she possibly stand it?

At Seven-thirty that evening, the nightshift workers of Demacio's Bistro were busy getting ready for the surge of dinnertime customers.

"Either of you counted up the change in the register?" The boss called out to his two part-time employees.

"I got it," called one, a teenage boy with a mop of red hair and several pimples. "It looks like you haven't been getting a lot of customers lately. What's been goin' on?"

The owner snorted and took a long drag on one of his favorite Cuban cigars. "What hasn't? For twenty-five years I've had to deal with that Thali's place up the road, which hogged half the people in the Goddamn city. And now the owners kicked the bucket, and suddenly people are too afraid to step outside of their own houses." He laughed, and his large stomach bounced. "You'd think it was vampires or something that killed 'em."

"Did you hear anything about what really killed them?"

"The report on the News said it was wolves. They got pretty badly torn up from what I heard. I guess they live out by the woods, or something. Their kid, too, if you can believe that." He shook his head, black curls bobbing. "Fifteen years old, that girl was. Crazy, eh?"

"But wouldn't wolves be too afraid of people to come that close? You don't hear about stuff like this too often."

"Exactly what I was thinkin'. Sounds more like some graphic homicide to me." Demacio took another long drag on his cigar. "Well, whatever happened, it's more profits for me. Reviera!" he called over his shoulder. "You got the tomato sauce for the pizzas stocked?"

"Comin' boss." An Hispanic man in his mid-to-late thirties appeared through the back door with two five-gallon drums of tomato sauce. "Which you want, Thyme and Basil, or Oregano?"

"Thyme and Basil," answered the boss. "And we need more Mozzarella back here, too."

"Gotcha, boss." Reviera went back out to the storage place.

Demacio turned back to see a customer in front of the counter, a young man of about twenty-one with blond hair and sunglasses, despite the fact that it was almost fully dark. "Can I help you?"

The customer removed his sunglasses. "I was wondering if you had a payphone? I've got to make a call. It's important."

"Back by the restrooms," said Demacio. The customer's eyes were eerie, sharp and hard as blue ice, and familiar. His gaze made the boss feel uneasy, and he wished the peculiar man would leave.

"Thank you. I haven't been able to afford one yet." The peculiar man headed back to the phone booths.

Demacio's beady black eyes watched him the whole way. "I don't like the looks of that guy," he muttered quietly to his teenage cashier. "He's trouble, all right, no two ways about it."

"You want me to kick him out?" asked the carrot topped boy.

"Nah, not yet. We'll see if he starts any funny business first." Demacio reached under the counter and fingered the .22 glock shotgun he kept for safety purposes. "We can handle funny business."

Kymbal, who had been leafing through the phone book, had heard the whispered conversation crystal-clear. *Cretins,* he fumed inwardly, scowling. *This is supposed to be private! I'll show them something to be afraid of!*

His eyes flashed red, and he muttered a whispered incantation in Romanian, gesturing towards them. Neither the boss nor the employee had any time to fathom what was going on before they both fell to the ground, out cold.

Smiling with satisfaction, the vampire turned back to the book. After he had flipped for a few more moments, he stopped in the right column. He ran a finger down the list of names until he found the one he was looking for. True to Garrison's word, it was very easy to find the name he was looking for.

"Here's my little firebrand," He said to himself. "I will have to remember to thank you, Garrison, you have been a greater help than you know." He pulled out an ornate pendant that held a strawberry-sized red crystal at the center. Gazing into the faceted depths, he smirked to himself.

Five minutes later, Anna Harper's telephone rang. With a sigh, she wiped away the tears in her eyes and picked it up.

"Hello?" she said, without much conviction.

"Hey, Anna," said Damien Roberson's voice on the other end. "What's up?"

Anna sat bolt upright, and her heart began to pound. She had not given Damien her phone number; where had he found it? Why was he calling now?

"What do you want?" she asked, putting just enough annoyance in her voice to let him know that she had not forgotten Saturday.

"Listen, I know you're probably totally peeved at me."

"You think?" This was so stupid, why had she even picked up?

"I don't know what came over me," he said. "I really like you a lot, Anna. I'm really sorry."

Anna was silent for several moments, thinking this all over. Her head was telling her not to trust a word Damien Roberson was saying, that the boy was dangerous somehow. So why couldn't she hang up?

"You mean it?" she finally inquired.

"Every word. Look, why don't we meet at Central Park and talk about this? I can be there in an hour. I want you to trust me, Anna, but that won't happen unless we both work at it."

Anna sighed. He *did* have a point there.

"I don't know," she responded blithely. "My dad might say no, he was really mad when I told him what happened."

"Ask him, please?"

"Okay, I'll ask. Goodbye." She hung up. "Dad? That was Damien. He said he wants to meet at Central Park to talk. In an hour."

"Are you sure you're up for it?" Her father asked. "You still look pretty flushed." He brushed a strand of blond hair out of her face.

"I'm fine. Besides, I think this is something I really need to do. I don't want one misunderstanding to ruin things for us."

"Okay. But I'm going to come with you. I don't trust that boy."

I couldn't agree more, Anna thought. She had, after all, promised Lysander that she would not go out at night alone.

An hour later Anna and her father pulled into Central Park.

"One hour, okay, Anna?" Her father asked.

"Yeah, okay." Anna shut the Pontiacs passenger door and walked towards the rosebush, where she could just make out Damien's tall, lean frame in the fast-approaching darkness.

"Glad you decided to come," he called out.

"Sure," she mumbled. "Look, Damien, can we keep this short? I'm feeling really run down."

"You mean because of Jennifer?" He put an arm around her shoulders. "Hey, it's okay. It was an accident, that's all."

As he pulled her close he nodded, just slightly, to Morugan, who was hidden in the trees. The Head Vampire's eyes began to glow, summoning the crystal from Anna's pocket into his hand. He cackled softly to himself.

"So are we okay?" Damien asked Anna, who noticed nothing except the way he held her; as gently as anything. Maybe he really did care about her; maybe what had transpired on Saturday really was just a misunderstanding.

"I guess," she sighed. "I shouldn't have blown up at you like that. You know, I hate to argue with people. There are so few who really care about me as it is."

"I don't blame you for reacting the way you did. I deserved it. I'm just glad you decided to give me a second chance."

"So am I."

"I guess it just happened because you're such a pretty girl," Damien said. "People do crazy things when they fall head over heels, you know?" He turned her to face him, grinning, and as he did so his eyes went from blue to a fiery, glowing red. At first Anna didn't realize he was trying to hypnotize her, but then she let out a scream and backed away.

"You're a vampire!"

It was all perfectly clear to her now; no wonder she only saw him at night, no wonder her mind went blank when he was near her, no wonder he felt dangerous. *I'm such an idiot*, she thought angrily.

His smile became a cold sneer. "Very perceptive. And my name isn't Damien, it's Darvis Kymbal. I confess myself impressed, you are very willful. But I always get what I'm after. Always."

"You killed Jennifer," Anna said, trembling. "It had to be you."

The sneer now became a frown. "I had no choice. She knew too much, I could not allow her to live. And, regretfully, I can neither allow you to live, now that the traitor has shown you who we are."

"Lysander," Anna murmured. Then she glared at him and shouted, "Where is he? What did you do to him?"

"Do not concern yourself with my nephew," called out a voice that cracked like a bolt of electricity, and the head vampire revealed himself. "You will soon be reunited, one last time. I must advise you not to run, it will prove quite futile."

He held up the crystal. He was so hideous with his chalk-white skin and bulging, ruby-red eyes that Anna could not stand to look at him. Instead her gaze wandered over to her father, who lay on the ground out cold. She was on her own now.

Suddenly Anna felt no fear at all, only white-hot anger. *"I will not run from you!"* She put to use her martial arts training, first tornado-kicking the Head Vampire, then firing a volley of punches, then kicking again. But just as she was about to punch one more time Kymbal seized her by the arms from behind and held on tightly.

Morugan laughed. "Impressive, for a human." He took her chin in one hand and raised her head up so they were eye-to-eye, although Anna shut hers instinctively. "And a fair little pixie you are, too. I can almost see why he would risk his life for you, girl." She struggled to free herself, but could not.

"Take her to the Manor," Morugan instructed. The head vampire flew off and Kymbal followed, holding onto their prisoner, who was screaming for all she was worth.

A few minutes later Mr. Harper awoke from his trance.

"Ugh. What a migraine," he muttered, shaking himself. "Let's go home." He looked around for his daughter but did not see her anywhere.

"Anna? Anna!"

Meanwhile, at a large house on Hayden Boulevard in the Bronx,

Lysander was struggling to free himself. He had managed to free his hands using a sharp stone on the floor of the cell, but getting out of the cell was another matter altogether. At the moment he was attempting to melt the bars with his fierce, fiery gaze, but all it was serving to do was give him a roaring headache.

"Very clever of you, Garrison, to put a Heat-Resistance spell on these bars," he grumbled, massaging his aching temples.

It was very hard for the vampire to concentrate on his predicament. For one thing, the place was awash with lights. Being artificial, they were not lethal to him as sunlight would be, but they were bright enough to be painful. And he kept hearing Kymbal's words in his mind.

Too bad Anna will never thank you for being a failure as a friend. I'll tell her goodbye for you.

The cruel words were punctuated by Anna's screams, echoing deafeningly in his mind. Was his dear friend even alive? He could not tell from this great of a distance where she was, or what was happening to her.

You damned fool; he chastised himself, *Just teleport out of here!* Lysander wasn't very good at teleportation yet, but it just might work if he concentrated hard on where he wanted to go. Let Kymbal say what he wanted; he would save his friend; one way or another.

Lysander focused on the outside of the cell with all his might. He found himself in the main hall where he could hear Garrison and his followers talking. From the sound of things, Kymbal had stolen the Firebrand. Well, so much the better for him now!

"That blood-sucking bastard was lying!" Garrison thundered. "The crystal was formed by the sun itself! We need to get it back. We need to get rid of them."

"So how do we get it back? All we have are minor spells."

"It'll be too difficult to do a surprise attack. They'll hear us coming five miles away."

"No it won't," Garrison said. "All we need is a spell to disguise ourselves, and we don't need the crystal for that."

"But who's gonna stand guard here?" Another hunter demanded. "The parasite might try to make a run for it."

"Do you mean me?" Lysander shouted. Quick as a flash, he immobilized one of the hunters, and then made a break for the door.

"Shoot the son of a bitch!" Garrison shouted. Three more of his followers aimed at Lysander, but he jumped out of the way. He immobilized another hunter, punched out two more that tried to seize him, then flew over the table and seized Garrison.

"I told you to leave Anna Harper alone," he snarled, with barely constrained fury.

"How the hell did you get loose?" Garrison asked in surprise.

"I would have thought you'd know better than to trust the undead by now." Throwing him roughly aside, the vampire went to the door. Just as he was about to step out, Garrison hurled a knife at him, just missing.

"You're too late, you goddamned freak," he spat, every syllable saturated with contempt. "You'll never see her again. She's dead."

Lysander's dark eyes flashed red, and the hunter was thrown backwards, knocked out cold. Then the vampire left.

Out on the street he walked past the other people trying to look as inconspicuous as possible. A few people shot him suspicious glances, but he mostly tried to think past the intense headache brought on by the bright shop lights and the highbeams of cars.

Which way was it to Manhattan? He remembered going in the opposite direction of Polaris. He looked up into the sky, but the stars were invisible from here, thanks to the streetlamps. So he continued walking on to the edge of town.

As he walked, he remembered the night that he had met Kari. He remembered her willingness to trust him when she knew he was a vampire. But how right had she really been? Or Anna, for that matter? His resolve had nearly given way at the sight of her. Who was to say how long it would last? After all, he was a vampire. He knew that there was only so much self-restraint a creature who needed the blood of others to survive could muster.

Stop it! He roared at himself. *You know you can't listen to Morugan. You're not him. Anna is your friend. So for Gods sake, act like it!*

Lysander had finally reached the end of town where it was mercifully dark. With a sigh, he looked around. No one was there, so he took flight. Looking up into the sky, he found Polaris and sailed toward it, as fast as he could.

Hold on, Anna, I'm coming.

Meanwhile back at the manor Morugan was listening. "So he managed to escape. Very clever. No matter, we will simply have to wait longer than anticipated." He turned to Anna, whose hands Kymbal was tying together behind her. "I shall enjoy draining your blood, girl. The hunt makes the kill more interesting, do you not agree?"

Anna scowled. "You are disgusting."

"I am merely providing for those who follow in my stead, as would any good leader," said the Head Vampire pristinely. "Surely you agree that without law there is no order, and without order there is no safety, and without safety there is death, nothing more."

"And what about all those people you're going to kill besides me? They have nothing to do with you. They don't even believe there are such things as vampires."

"I do not wish to take chances. Trust was what cost me my freedom, my family, my good name. I have attempted time and again, for nearly eight centuries, to set it to rights, and have gone through torments you could not imagine. I know more than anyone the foolishness of trust."

Anna snorted in annoyance. "Oh man, are you ever pathetic. What could I do by myself? I'm just one kid!"

"Anna, sweetheart, try to understand," Kymbal said in a smooth voice. "Lysander broke the rules. These are hard times for our kind. There is no room for insubordination." He moved in closer and graced her cheek with one hand, which made the girl gasp in pain. "It only takes a few seconds. You won't feel a thing. Don't be afraid."

Anna wasn't afraid, she was angry. Lysander had been nothing but good to her. He did not deserve to be killed, and she was in no mood to let herself become Vampire Fruit Punch, either. Discreetly, she fished her penknife out of her pocket-which was no easy trick-and in a matter of seconds she had freed her hands and was ready to fight.

"Feel this!" She punched a swift uppercut, and then followed up with a tornado kick that drove the vampire back.

She dashed to the front of the room and swiped the yellow gemstone from the altar. No sooner had she done so than Morugan seized her arm in a tight, burning grip. She screamed in pain.

"Going somewhere, girl?" He sneered. "There is no escape."

Anna brought up her other fist and punched the Head Vampire with all the strength she possessed. Then she stomped his foot and ran for the door.

"Come back here, you *grike!*" he shouted as the girl careened down the corridor and out of sight as fast as her lithe frame would go. He knew she would smash the gemstone, ruin everything. Why hadn't he killed her on first sight?

"Go get her!" he snarled at Kymbal in Romanian, and the younger vampire took off after Anna.

Anna careened around a corner and down the stairs, looking for a place to stop and destroy the crystal. But where? There was nothing but dark walls softly lit by torches for what seemed like miles.

She passed the ballroom, the study, and a pair of doors that were locked-probably a broom closet, although vampires weren't much for cleanliness. The whole place seemed to be covered in dust and cobwebs.

I am never going to Cental Park at night again, Anna thought furtively as she ran. *I've had it with this vampire crap.*

Finally Anna saw a large room that had a variety of swords and knives and other weapons on the walls. The Armory. She ran inside.

Looks like as good a place as any to destroy an evil crystal, she thought. At least here there were better tools than her small penknife to do the work.

Anna looked around. Finally her gaze landed on a big, thick-bladed battle axe. "No way that won't work," she said to herself. She walked over and picked up the axe. Balancing it carefully-it was very heavy- Anna threw the flashing crystal to the ground.

"Here goes nothing." Anna raised the axe high, then brought it down with a loud, thudding *Crack!* onto the floor. Immediately, there was an explosion of light so bright Anna was forced to close her eyes. When she opened them again the crystal lay cut cleanly in half.

Anna smiled, satisfied. There. She had kept her promise to her friend. *Now I've gotta get out of here and find Lysander. I wonder where the hunters are keeping him?* She went for the door when Kymbal's voice suddenly rang out into the silence.

"Well done, Anna. Round one to you." The vampire dropped down from the ceiling. "Unfortunately, you won't be going anywhere."

Anna was so stunned that she dropped the axe. It clattered noisily to the floor. "What do you want with me, you freak?" Her voice was firm, but inside she was water. "What do you want? Tell me right now!"

"You know very well why we have you here." Kymbal's blue eyes flashed, colder than an arctic glacier. "Don't try to play Cat and Mouse with me. I tire of this foolishness."

"Believe me, I am sick to death of being the mouse." Anna glared at him, and a flume of fire suddenly erupted between them.

Anna gasped in surprise. *Did I do that?* She wondered, awestruck. *Did I get some weird power when I destroyed the crystal?*

There was no time to wonder. She stared down the vampire and continued, in ringing tones, "I'm sick of you bothering Lysander." She raised her hand up, and another, larger, trail of fire shot from her palm towards Kymbal. He leaped out of the way. "I'm sick of going to school to find another of my friends has been killed." She released fire rings at the vampire, which he also dodged. "And I'm *really* sick of being burned!" She clenched her fist, forming a large fireball, and then released it.

Kymbal glared at her. The little brat! If she had hit him, he would have been incinerated. But the expression of outrage lasted for only a moment. Then he sneered at her again. He wasn't out of his league just yet, after all.

"I see you are proving to be quite the firecracker." He gestured upward, and she rose into the air, caught in a paralyzing grip. "This makes things more interesting, doesn't it?" He grabbed her arm and pulled her towards himself, which made the girl scream in agony as she never had before. "But what do you say we cool off for a bit."

He placed a hand to the girl's chest and muttered an incantation. At first she gasped in pain at his touch, but then her breathing grew shallower. Her stiffly tensed muscles went limp, and her eyes closed as he slowed her heart rate gradually until she had lost consciousness.

The vampire caught her in his arms. "Guilt through association is guilt all the same, my love." He sighed. "Why must you do everything the hard way?"

He sent a mental message to the Head Vampire. *I have overpowered the girl. What shall we do with her?*

Into the Icebox, was the reply. *Children's blood is better chilled.*

Kymbal snickered. With a wave of his hand he mended the crystal. He picked it up, and his smile grew wider as he watched it flash. "As you wish, Master." And he left with the girl in his arms and the crystal clenched in his fist.

VI
"Watch Over Her."

Thirty minutes later Lysander entered the suburbs of Manhattan, Anna's neighborhood. Upon arriving at his friend's house, the vampire found not her, but her father, pulling into the driveway with a grim expression on his face.

"Mr. Harper," He shouted, "Mr. Harper, wait!"

The man turned around, frowning. "What do you want?"

"Anna's gone, isn't she?"

Mr. Harper sighed. "I don't know where she is. We went to Central Park so she could smooth over a misunderstanding with a boy friend of hers. I was listening, and then all of a sudden I just dropped to the ground in a faint. When I came out of it she was gone. I looked all over town, I can't find her anywhere."

Lysander's eyes narrowed. "That boy. He took her."

"Took her?"

"Yes. At the clan's insistence. They had a deal with the hunters, me for her."

Anna's father snorted. "And why should I believe that you're not in on this? You're a vampire; you could be lying to me right now."

"Well, I'm not." Lysander's eyes flashed angrily, but did not hypnotize. "I don't care if you trust me, but Anna does. She's in danger, and I know where she is. I'm not going to fail her. We're wasting time, now are you with me or not?"

And for the first time Mr. Harper saw him for what he truly was; not a fearful demon of the night, but an honest young man who loved his daughter as much as he did himself.

"Of course I am, this is my daughter we're talking about."

"We must go now," Lysander said. "She's growing weaker the longer we wait."

"Where did they take her?"

"Bluerock Manor. That's where the clan lives. It's just outside the city."

Mr. Harper started the Pontiac's engine. "Come on, let's go."

The two arrived at Bluerock Manor half an hour later.

"Interesting," Mr. Harper said, walking over to the twelve-foot fence that encircled the mansion.

He reached out a hand to begin climbing, but Lysander shouted, "No, don't!"

Anna's father drew his hand back.

"It's cursed," The vampire explained. "You won't be able to climb that."

"Why am I not surprised?" Mr. Harper sighed in frustration. "So how do we get in?"

"There's an old Roma incantation," Lysander said thoughtfully, pacing. "I remember. Yes, that's it. You might want to stand back."

Mr. Harper stood back.

Lysander began to chant in his native language, a rapid, methodic incantation that echoed in the night. The young vampire's eyes began to glow red, and the gate began to wretch and buck, almost as if it were alive.

Suddenly he shouted, in English, "Get down! Don't let your eyes connect!"

Taken a little aback at this abrupt command, Mr. Harper ducked nonetheless.

The gate gave one final wretch, then spat its cracked lock at Lysander, who said, "Thank you, you have been very cooperative." He started up the walk, followed by Anna's utterly frazzled father.

"Whose bright idea was it to put up a security system like that, anyway?" Mr. Harper demanded.

"Morugan`s. The Head of the clan. And it gets worse form here, believe me."

Soon the two were walking through the elaborate main hall, carpeted in Midnight blue and softly lit by torches in brackets along the stone walls. Lysander pulled one of the torches from its bracket and held it aloft as he proceeded through the mansion.

"Come on, we need to get to the dungeons."

A large Black Widow spider came out of the darkness and scuttled across Mr. Harper's feet. He gave a low gasp of horror and sank back away from it.

"Are you sure this is the right way?"

"Positive. Don't dawdle."

The two went down a winding staircase, lighting the way with the brackets. Soon it led to a variety of catacombs deep under the Manor. Mr. Harper noticed that cobwebs hung from every crevice, and shuddered, trying not to imagine their inhabitants.

HEEEEKKK! Suddenly a loud hiss interrupted his thoughts.

"Um, I don't think we're alone in here!"

A trio of gigantic spiders, six feet long at least, skittered out from the darkness. Their long pincers clicked menacingly as they rushed after the two intruders.

Anna's father tensed. He was a master of Martial arts and had taught Anna all she knew, but his skills had never been tested like this. And he knew that if he failed he would lose his daughter forever.

Just as one of the beasts came rushing upon him he connected his foot with its jowls in a swift movement, then threw an uppercut that sent it sprawling away on spindly legs.

Incensed, the arachnid shrieked and revved up on its hind legs, and grasped the man's leg in its pincers. It tugged viciously, like an angry attack dog.

Mr. Harper dug around desperately in his pocket, and pulled out his pocket knife. Summoning all his grit, he plunged the three-inch blade into the spider's abdomen. A considerable amount of what might have been the creature's blood-only it was the color and consistency of battery acid- leaked out over the floor. He leapt out of the way as the substance scalded the floor.

Meanwhile Lysander was fending off his own assailant. The arachnid was spitting venom at the vampire as he attempted to immobilize it with a red-eyed glare. He leapt backwards onto a dais and hissed warningly at the creature.

"Back off," he hissed in Romanian.

His glare intensified- it was difficult to penetrate all eight of a spider's eyes- and he shouted a curse in Romanian.

Instead of falling to the floor, however, the spider merely shrieked with anger. It snapped its pincers within inches of the young vampire, nearly missing him. Lysander jumped up to a rafter in the ceiling and repeated the curse, focusing even harder. Finally, the spider dropped to the floor.

There, thought Lysander, jumping to the ground. *Even Morugan would have been impressed by that.*

There was no time too celebrate, however. No sooner had the second beast been defeated than the third came charging at Mr. Harper. He just managed to jump out of the way before a pincer snapped around his ankle.

"Any ideas?"

The spider spat a glob of venom at the two intruders.

Lysander jumped up and away from the arachnid.

"Get ready to trip it up," He called down to Mr. Harper. "I'll immobilize it."

Mr. Harper tensed; waiting for the opportune moment as the spider skittered nearer, clicking its pincers. He knew the arachnid would kill him if he miscalculated even in the slightest.

It was almost upon him now. He looked into its eight shiny eyes.

Now! He lashed out his foot and knocked the spider's legs out from underneath it. He sucker punched the creature, then spun on his heel and gave a roundhouse kick to its bulging abdomen. And still the creature continued to writhe. He gripped onto its pincers tightly to keep its poisonous jaws from biting him.

"You might want to paralyze this thing right about now!"

Just then the creature gave an almighty thrash and sent the man flying. He landed hard against a pillar, but merely shook off the impact, then rushed back at the spider.

"Don't!" Lysander's eyes blazed red, and he uttered the paralyzing spell for the third time that night. Instantly, the creature dropped to the floor, out cold.

"We should get out of here; the spell won't hold it for long."

"No need," Mr. Harper said. Swift as a hawk he brought the silver blade slicing down through the air and plunged it into the spider's abdomen. Once more the black, acidic substance bubbled out of the creature.

Lysander realized with surprise that his respect for Anna's father had grown considerably. The man had fought bravely and cleverly, never hesitating.

"Good work."

"You, too." Mr. Harper looked around. "So now where do we go?"

"This way." The vampire set off briskly for the opposite end of the catacombs, towards a pair of doors.

Now the two found themselves inside a room that was kept magically frozen.

"She's in here. I can feel it." Lysander looked around for the girl and finally saw her, lying perfectly still at the other end of the room. She was nearly as white as paper, and seemed to hardly be breathing.

"Anna!" Mr. Harper was running towards her when all of a sudden an enormous gray timber wolf came bounding out of nowhere, snarling furiously, its yellow eyes wild. With an angry roar, it rose up on its hind legs and pushed Mr. Harper, knocking him to the floor.

"Get away!" He struggled futilely to pull the large wolf off, but it was incredibly strong and refused to budge.

"Silence!" the creature growled in a deep, barking rasp. "You shall trespass no further."

"Vlad, get off of him," Lysander said impatiently.

"The-the wolf can talk?" Mr. Harper sputtered; both from shock and the pressure of the wolf's large paws.

"Yes, he can talk. He just never has anything worthwhile to say."

"Silence!" Vlad barked, louder than before. "You shall *not* trespass upon the property of Master Morugan!"

"We- we're not here to trespass," Mr. Harper gasped. At these words the wolf's ears pricked up, and he got off of his quarry. Mr. Harper stood, shivering from the cold ground.

"Is that so, mortal scum? Do tell me the nature of your business here."

"We're only here for my daughter," Mr. Harper said. "That little girl over there." He gestured to his daughter, lying unconscious and dangerously near death at the opposite end of the room. "Will you let us get her out of here?"

Vlad turned and gave the girl a long, hard look. His ears flattened. Then he began to pace, his thick tail swishing on the ground.

"Hmm. Master Morugan is frightfully powerful. You are a traitorous rogue and a weak human. What incentive do I have to allow you your little lost pup?"

"I will turn you into a fur pelt, obstinate beast." Lysander's eyes flashed a fearful shade of red, just for a second.

The wolf laughed a harsh, ugly sound. "You jest, boy."

"Very well. You have been warned." Lysander's eyes began to glow red. Muttering fiercely in Romanian, he focused on the wolf's legs. The creature flew backwards and hit the stone wall hard. Lysander gestured upward, and the wolf hit the ceiling. Then he came crashing down to the floor.

Vlad stood and shook himself off. "You have grit, boy," he said, laughing. "I had no idea you could will yourself into acting so violently. You always struck me as being too weak-hearted."

"You confuse compassion with weakness," The vampire said vehemently. "Now stand aside or I will give you worse."

"She'll die if she stays in here," Mr. Harper said earnestly. "Please, let her go."

"Hrrrr, I do indeed love a good negotiation," the wolf growled. "But we deal on *my* terms. Give me the answers I seek, and I will let you pass. Answer wrongly, and I tear you to bits."

"Very well," Lysander sighed. "Get on with it."

"Tell me what shines like diamonds bright
But is worth a thousand times more
Icy and harsh as an arctic glacier
Vast as the sea from the distant shore.
Tell me what is warm as a candle flame
Drawing out those who go their way alone
The everlasting talisman that leads the traveler home."

Why did I agree to this ridiculous creature's terms?
Lysander wondered angrily. *We don't have time for this. We need to get Anna out of here right now. I should have blasted that crazy fleabag to bits when I first saw him.*

Just then Mr. Harper spoke. "The night sky. It's the night sky that leads travelers home. Polaris."

"You are correct, mortal." The wolf trotted over to the other end of the room and sat on his haunches, all the while keeping his eerie eyes on the pair of them. "Retrieve the girl now. And be quick about it; your presence is not welcome here."

Lysander quickly knelt beside his friend and raised her head up. The girl was cold as death, and he wondered for a moment if they were too late.

In an instant Mr. Harper was by their side. "Anna, wake up, honey, come on." He shook her shoulder gently, but she did not stir.

"What's wrong with her?" Mr. Harper asked, looking the vampire right in the eye.

Lysander took the girl's hand in his own. He could feel a very slight pulse, although he knew the enchantment had certainly been intended to kill his friend. How fortunate that they had not wasted more time arguing!

"She's been put under an enchantment. Her heart rate's been slowed."

"She's not...?" Mr. Harper could not finish the sentence.

"No, she's not dead. I know of a draught that can revive her."

"Thank God." Mr. Harper sighed in relief.

"We've got to get her to someplace warm." The vampire stood with Anna in his arms and strode for the door. "Follow me. I know a place where you'll be safe."

Mr. Harper followed, into a corridor, down the hall to the left, and finally they stopped in a room off the Armory.

This room was very different from the others. It was no better lit than the rest of the rooms, but somehow less creepy. Cleaner and welcoming, with a vast array of plants.

Lysander laid Anna down at the fountain and found her pulse. Her heart rate had weakened further still, and he knew he had only minutes to save his friend. He took off his jacket and pulled it over her to warm her, then set to work.

He took water from the fountain and hurriedly began collecting herbs. Tamarind, Marjoram, Asphodel, Fuganeek. He expertly crushed and mixed them, then set them to boil in a pot that had been bubbling over the hearth.

"You're a very strange vampire," Mr. Harper said, watching him work hurriedly. "Why would you rather save a little girl's life than suck her blood?"

"I told you before, all vampires are not equal. I just so happen to be an enemy of the monsters that did this to Anna."

"You are?"

"Of course, why do you think I've been keeping my distance from this damned place?"

Lysander poured the drought into a glass and sat beside Anna. With a surgeon's careful efficiency, he raised her head up and lifted the glass to her mouth.

"Come on, Anna, drink. You have to pull through."

She began to drink, very slowly.

"That's it. That's it, darling." Lysander stroked her blond waves, looking at her with all the love in the world. He did not want to leave, but he knew what he had to do, and delaying would only make it that much more difficult. He knew he would never see her again.

"Anna said you're a good healer," Mr. Harper spoke up.

"That's right, I am a healer. Not a killer." Lysander grinned cheerlessly, revealing flawless white teeth, as he went to the door.

"Watch over her. She'll be okay now."

"Where are you going?"

"I have a score to settle with the master." With that the vampire left.

Mr. Harper took Lysander's place at his daughter's side with a weary sigh.

Lysander strode purposefully through the corridors to the Armory, his dark eyes flashing.

"*Morugan!*" he shouted in Romanian, his voice thunderous. "Get out here! *Now!*"

Suddenly the Head Vampire appeared, surrounded by six or seven cronies. "Why, Lysander," he purred, smiling in a very frightening way. "We thought you dead by now. Pray tell, how *did* you escape?"

"I tapped into my ancestry, of course. It would appear that you have let be known too much for your own good, *Master.*"

Lysander spoke the last word with all the contempt in the world.

Morugan's face darkened immediately. "Insolent wretch!" He summoned a Machete from the Armory wall. "We will see what you are capable of!"

Lysander summoned a sword. "I'm not afraid of you!" And Uncle and Nephew began to trade blows.

"You dare mock *me*?" Morugan ranted. "I took you in when you had nothing, boy. I raised you as though you were my own son. Taught you everything you needed to know. Apparently my generosity was wasted on you. You are no better than those weakling daywalkers you are so fond of!" He swung viciously at his surrogate nephew.

"Generosity! Ha!" Lysander parried the blow and returned it with equal vehemence. "I seem to recall that it was *you*, Morugan, who made me into what I am. You took me from my home. From my family. From my life. You imposed upon me a lifetime of seclusion in this Godforsaken place." The young vampire's words flowed hotter and faster, as did his blows. "There is nothing generous about you at all."

"Without me you would not stand a chance!" Morugan hissed, his machete slicing though the air before the handle plunged into Lysander, causing the youth to double over. "Foolish, ridiculous, perpetually stubborn boy!" He raised the machete over his nephew, ready to behead him in one stroke. "You would have been well served to die along with the absurd family you so cherish in memorandum."

"Better death than to be a fiend!" Lysander kicked the machete out of Morugan's hand and got back to his feet. "I'm not you, Morugan." He pointed his own blade at the Head Vampire, forcing him slowly backward. "I have a heart. I have a vow to fulfill. And I have had enough of being abused by you and your slaves!"

The rest of the vampires hissed and shouted threateningly, but Lysander paid no attention to them. For once he had the Head Vampire right where he wanted him.

Meanwhile in the Atrium, Anna's eyes snapped open. "Dad?"

She sat up slowly, feeling a pounding migraine. Damn vampires!

"Are you okay, Anna?" Her father hugged her.

"I'm fine." She looked around. The place seemed comfortingly familiar, but she knew it was not Lysander's hideout in Central Park. "Where are we?"

"The vampires took you," said Mr. Harper, who was still turning to jelly inside at the thought of what would have happened to his daughter if he had not trusted Lysander. "I thought you were dead."

"Lysander must have brought you to this place."

"I had to trust him. I had to get you somewhere safe." Mr. Harper stroked her blond hair, his face awash with relief.

"We can't stay here, we have to fight." Anna stood up and went for the door.

"Anna, where are you going?"

"To find my friend. He needs my help."

"No. Anna, *no*."

"I have to."

"They're *vampires*," Mr. Harper insisted. "We can't get in the way of dueling vampires, they'll kill us."

"I can try." Anna's eyes blazed like green fire, hot and dangerous. In the dim light she resembled her mother more than ever. "I'm not afraid of them."

And before Mr. Harper could say anything more, Anna was gone.

Meanwhile the vampires were still swinging away at one another.

"I see that I have underestimated your will," Morugan cackled. "It never dawned on me that you would dare fight the Head Vampire in his own lair. It is a pity indeed that I will have to make an end of you, boy."

Lysander hissed. "You can no more control me with the sword than the hunters could with the cell, old hellhound. I'll not obey you, not ever!"

Morugan snarled angrily. "Insolent wretch...." But his epithet was cut off mid-rant as the subtle scent of young blood-sweet to the taste, and invigorating, besides-caught his attention. It was that girl. The foolhardy little minx was approaching. So he had not stopped her heart with his magic. Never mind, there were other ways to turn the tide in his favor. A wicked fanged smile came over his face as a plan formed in his mind, even as he fought.

"Can't control you, can I? Won't do my bidding will you? I know you better than you are willing to admit. A weakling whose anger and sentimentality have been the root cause behind his every failure and his ultimate undoing."

Lysander swung his sword with all his strength, and was met with a clash of metal against metal. "I will show you how weak I am!"

"You intend to kill me?" asked Morugan, jumping up onto the wall, the evil smile never wavering. "Is that what you are planning to do? You have neither the gall nor the wit." He was met with faster, harder blows, but parried and returned them calmly and methodically. "After all, how long did that pathetically weak human girl take to awaken when you accidentally hypnotized her? Thirty seconds, perhaps? That was not even a hint of your true potential. I wonder what your friend would say if she knew?"

"That is no business of yours, Morugan!" Lysander hissed. "Leave the girl out of it, she is an innocent. This is between you and me."

"But I speak the truth." Morugan jumped away farther down the wall "And one must wonder why you did such a thing; placed someone whom you call a friend under such an enchantment. You are a vampire, Lysander. A stealthy, elusive hunter, as I am. Deny it all you wish, but you have no friends. You have no desire for them."

"Enough!" Lysander's eyes flashed red as he drove his surrogate uncle back. "I won't listen to your mind games!"

"No one ever said this was a game, Lysander." Morugan gestured upward, and his nephew rose into the air towards him, caught tight in the enchantment. "I am dead serious. This is the last time you will ever disobey me, boy." He brought his nephew over to him and twisted the youth's arm behind him in a half-nelson. Then the old vampire began to murmur an old incantation, one that was nearly unheard of, in his native language.

Vampires were capable of terrible things. They could punish others, could injure or even kill with their magic. However, using magic to control the minds of others was considered perhaps the blackest sin of all. As vampires were typically made through the bite of another, they vowed to never addle with free will. And addling was exactly what Morugan was doing with his nephew's free will. His followers gave out gasps of surprise, and some even hissed, as Morugan's ruby-colored eyes flashed. Lysander roared with pain. He struggled frantically to get loose, but his uncle had an iron grip on him. He could feel a black pit opening up inside him, filling him with anger and hatred.

"That's it, that's it, boy!" Morugan hissed in his ear excitedly. "Let your rage consume you as a fire destroys a forest and all the creatures within. Give full vent to the darkness that resides inside you. Use the sinister powers that are yours to unleash. You are a vampire, a vampire!"

Finally, he let go of the youth. With his eyes flashing red, hissing through his long fangs, Lysander hardly resembled the kind young man Anna Harper had come to love. He looked like a vampire, a terrifying, deadly vampire. With a furious snarl, he rounded on Morugan and immediately let loose such a crippling bolt of electricity at his surrogate uncle that the elder doubled over on impact.

The other vampires hissed at him, shouted insults and Padmona ran out to attack him. "No one touches the master!" She swung at him with an ax, and was met with a crash of metal on metal.

"Get out of my way," Lysander snarled, "or you will die as well!"

He returned the blow, and thus began yet another row amidst the vampires.

Kymbal was alarmed. He sidled up to the Head Vampire and said, "My lord, what was the purpose of turning him? I thought we were intending to kill him."

"That we will indeed do," Morugan replied, another grin coming over his pallid lips. "However, we will wait for him to kill the girl first. I do think that since they were such friends, it is only fair that they should die together."

VII
"He's Out Of Control!"

Meanwhile Anna was running through the corridors. She could feel Lysander's presence within the mansion, but had no idea where to look for him. She pelted up a staircase, then rounded a corner, and stopped to catch her breath.

She could hear a haunting howl from somewhere to her left. It sounded frighteningly like a wolf.

Anna shuddered. She hated wolves. Large dogs had always scared her to death. She put one hand into her pocket, and her fingers bumped against her penknife. Well, she was pretty sure Lysander had gotten past worse than this to find her.

Griping the knife tightly, she turned another corner. There she found herself face to face with a giant gray timber wolf. It snarled at the girl, yellow eyes mad, and then jumped at her.

With a loud shriek, she jumped out of the way. The creature slid clumsily across the floor, hit a wall, and then turned back to the girl, growling even more furiously. "Do not think of running. You are afraid. You will not get five meters."

"I am not afraid, fleabag." Anna didn't look it, but she was surprisingly strong for someone as small as she was. And she was ready this time. As the big dog lunged at her again she kicked at the creature, and knocked it down. She walked over to the fallen animal and stabbed it with her penknife.

"I will tear you to bits for that!" The wolf grabbed her ankle in its teeth and dragged her to the ground.

Anna screamed as the needle-sharp teeth dug into her flesh, deeper and deeper. Through the haze of pain, one idea only came to her. If this did not work, nothing would....

She drew back her other foot, then brought it crashing down upon the wolf's head. Then she gestured quickly, and let loose an enormous fireball that incinerated the creature on contact.

"Fat chance, fleabag."

Anna sat up slowly and examined the wound. It was deeper than she had thought, and bleeding profusely. She knew that she needed to stop it right away, or she would certainly die. But how?

Then an idea came to her; if the sun could destroy, could it not also heal?

She placed her hands over the spot and felt it grow warm on contact. The bleeding slowed, and eventually stopped as the wound grew shallower and shallower, while she watched in amazement. Finally, her leg was completely healed.

There, she thought, gingerly standing up and testing her strength. Lysander would have been proud to see that.

Where *was* he?!

She stood back up and listened hard. She could hear Lysander's shouts, but where were they coming from? This place had more twists and turns than a funhouse! Then she knew;

He's in the Armory, She thought. Of course. *Boy, am I stupid!*

She started running, but hadn't gone more than ten feet when a large hand grabbed her.

"Well, well, well, this is turning out to be a very interesting night, isn't it?" sneered the man who had grabbed her. It was the charlatan who had menaced Lysander, and her as well.

"I never thought I'd see the day when you would willingly destroy the bloodsucker's guard dog. I thought you were their friend."

"Friend?" Anna spat. "My best friend was Jennifer Mendez. They killed her. I wouldn't side with them to save my own life!"

"Is that so? Then what about that boy you're so fond of? He's one of them."

"He is *not!*" hissed Anna. "He has been nothing but good to me. You might have noticed that by the fact that I'm still alive."

"Don't mean a thing," the hunter said. "They always mess with people before they kill 'em. That's their nom-du-plumb. And I hate to break it to you, sweetheart, but that's just what he's done to you. You'd know it for yourself if you could see him right about now."

"I'm going to him right now," she fumed, wresting herself from his grasp. "I'm going to help him. That's what friends do." And she ran off for the armory.

Garrison wasn't about to let her get away. He muttered a simple incantation, and Anna fell to the ground, momentarily paralyzed.

"No one's going to get there before me. I came here to destroy those abominations of nature, and that's what I'm going to do. See ya around, sweetheart."

Anna glared and let loose a barrage of fireballs right at the cretins' feet. "Oh no, you don't."

He yelled loudly and rolled around frantically, trying to stomp out the blaze. Meanwhile, the spell holding Anna in place broke, and she quickly stood up.

"All that's going to happen is those vampires are going to suck you bone-dry, just like they did to Jennifer. You can't beat them, and you know it."

"So, you wanna fight with magic, do you?" Garrison snarled. "Fine, then, show me what you can do, you little brat." He gestured upward, and Anna flew up into the air and hit the ceiling hard. He gestured downward, and she plummeted to the floor with a bone-wrenching crash. He gestured up again and then down.

Up and down, up and down, over and over. He grinned wickedly, clearly enjoying the sport.

"I've been hunting these damn things since before you were born. I know more magic than you can possibly imagine."

He gestured to the left, and Anna slid across the floor until she hit the wall hard. The girl did not cry out, she merely spat out a mouthful of blood and glared at the hunter.

"You know what? I won't give them the opportunity. They won't kill you tonight, I will."

He pulled her up roughly by the arm and held tightly with one hand, and pulled out his pocket knife with the other." He pulled her head back and brought the knife to her neck, ready to run her through.

Just then Anna elbowed him in the gut so hard that he dropped the weapon and doubled over in pain. Taking advantage of her assailant's momentary weakness, she kicked as hard as she could and broke free of his grasp. Anna dashed away from him, and quickly made a desperate gesture. Immediately she formed her biggest fireball yet, and let it loose at the hunter. He yelled in anguish as the fire consumed him. Nothing but ashes was left when the fire died out.

"Guess again, loony."

She ran as fast as she could for the Armory. She had to find Lysander *now*! This time he was the one who needed her.

In the armory, Padmona and Lysander crashed blades, and then broke apart. As they were equally matched for strength, both vampires were now becoming weak from the continuous fighting.

"I told you to get out of my way," Lysander snarled.

"Never! Master Morugan will be forever grateful to me for having killed you right here!" Padmona swung one more time, and knocked the sword from Lysander's hand. "There is no room for you here among us, traitor."

"No room for you, you mean."

Quickly, he gestured, and the other vampire was consumed by fire instantly.

Garrison took Padmona's place. He was particularly good at teleportation, and vanished every few moments, reappearing just long enough to blast Lysander with a furious gale, sending him crashing into the walls over and over.

"Coward!" Lysander bellowed, loud enough to rattle the windows. "Stand and fight, if you dare!"

The other zoomed in and sliced into Lysander. Then he dashed off, zoomed back in, and sliced into him again. He disappeared again, and knocked the other vampire down. And just as quickly, he was gone again. Only his voice could be heard, echoing around the room. "You are pathetic!" And he laughed like a maniac.

Lysander roared. He sent a wild current of electricity around the room.

Suddenly there was the other vampire, lying motionless on the floor. He struggled up to a sitting position, his face livid.

"You will pay for that!" He fired a ball of kinetic energy back at Lysander, which he dodged just in time.

Lysander gestured and muttered a death curse, and the other vampire was also consumed by flames.

At this very moment Anna entered the room. She gasped aloud, hardly daring to believe what her eyes were seeing. It shook her to her foundations, it really did.

"Oh, Lysander, what did he do to you?"

It was an enchantment, she was sure of it. Lysander would never show such blatant disregard for any life, not even that of his enemies. She had seen it in his heart. She didn't care what anyone said.

We're all doomed if someone doesn't stop him, She realized. *Well, maybe I can. He's healed me. Maybe I can heal him from the darkness that's poisoned him.*

Anna realized, of course, that she would more likely than not be killed in the attempt, but somehow the idea did not frighten her. There were worse things.

She gripped the penknife in her hand tighter.

Just then her father ran up behind her.

"Anna," he said firmly, "Whatever you're thinking about doing right now, forget it. I will not allow you to put yourself in the middle of this fight. It doesn't concern us."

"Yes, it does. He is my friend. I am not going to abandon him."

"I don't want these creatures to take my daughter from me." Mr. Harper put a hand on Anna's shoulder. "I already lost your mother," he said, and the stern, reprimanding tone was gone from his voice. He spoke with nothing but sorrow, and such pain that she could barely stand to hear it. "I can't go through that again; it would kill me for sure."

"Dad, look at him," Anna said, gesturing to her friend-her only friend now- who had resumed his assault on the Head Vampire. "He's out of control. If he carries on like this he'll destroy everyone, me included. I'm not going to let that happen to him. Or," she added, turning to meet his gaze, "to my father. I have to at least try."

And before her father could say another word, she was running as fast as she could towards the fray.

Of course, Morugan saw her. "Now!" he thundered at Kymbal in Romanian as he struggled to fight, "Get the girl!"

Kymbal drifted over to her and grabbed her wrist, grinning evilly. "Anna, darling, how good to see you were able to join the night's festivities."

"Yeah, too bad I can't honestly say the same."

"That's not very nice."

"Oh really?" She wretched her hand free and punched him hard. "Well, neither is lying." She punched again. "It isn't nice to deceive people." She kicked at him. "Or to destroy innocent lives."

She continued to pummel him. "I can't believe I trusted you, I don't know *what* I was thinking." And with that she turned and started to walk away.

"It's bad manners to run away when someone wants to talk to you." Kymbal gestured upward and Anna flew back over to him, paralyzed. He grabbed her and held on tightly so she couldn't escape.

"You know," Kymbal hissed in her ear, "I really didn't want to have to kill Jennifer just to keep our little secret. She was sweet. Not an uncooperative fighter like you. It never would have had to happen if you hadn't stubbornly insisted on seeing more of what shouldn't have been seen at all. You were so desperate to have a friend that you took a chance with a potentially fatal being. And now look at him." He grasped her chin in one hand and raised her head up, forcing her to look at the fierce battle before them.

"That is exactly how your friendship with him will end, with your death by his hands, right now." He applied a crushing grip to her wrist, and she gasped in pain. "It's really not so surprising that you were so fond of Lysander. You are both far too stubborn to heed advice and know what's good for you." And he began to drag her over to the dueling vampires.

No, Anna thought fiercely, *I will not die like this!*

"Yep," she said breezily. "You're right. But I do know how to fight." With that she elbow hooked him so hard that he doubled over. Then she let loose an unrelenting barrage of fire rings until Darvis Kymbal was completely incinerated.

Anna turned and continued to run towards her friend. "Lysander, stop! You don't know what you're doing, this isn't you!"

As she got closer she could feel herself getting weaker, walking slower and slower, but she kept going. Finally she was only inches from him.

"Lysander, listen to me. You are my friend." She grasped his hand like she had done the first night they met. "You will be my friend forever, no matter what." By now she was so weak that her legs were threatening to give way beneath her. She shut her eyes tightly, but did not let go. A soft red flame formed around her small hand as she grasped his.

"Leave me!" Lysander roared, wrenching out of her grasp, and he sent her reeling to the floor between himself and the Head Vampire. She hit the floor with a bone-wrenching thud, and did not move again. His pulsating red eyes bored into her with a great enough intensity to kill her.

Yet, even as she hit the floor, her voice was still echoing in his ears. Morugan`s mad laughter reverberated around the large room, but Lysander could hear only the words of the girl who-for all he knew-was dead already. Suddenly his eyes went back to brown, and he saw what he had done.

"Anna!" Mr. Harper was running towards his daughter, past caring about anything else. Lysander knew the man would certainly be killed if the Head Vampire got near him. Not a moment too soon, he reached out and pulled Anna's father back.

"Get back!"

"Let me go, she's hurt!"

"You softhearted fool," sneered Morugan. "You thought you were a match for me. The most powerful vampire on earth. You thought you could not be bent to my will. And now just look what you have done."

"Stay away from her, old demon!" Lysander shouted.

"Hmph. She is dead already. Thanks to you and your foolishness. And now you, my dear pathetic nephew, will never see the light of day again." He strode past Anna and knocked Lysander down with one powerful blow to the midsection with the handle of the machete. "Tonight you die, wretch, as I should have seen to right from the beginning." He raised the machete, ready to kill.

However, at that very moment, Lysander grabbed the knife Anna had dropped. Quick as lightning, he reached up and plunged it into his uncle's heart, before he could be harmed by the machete. The head vampire let out one long, loud shriek of pain-riddled fury, then vanished in a black storm cloud. One by one, his followers were similarly destroyed. Only ashes were left in their wake.

With the clan defeated, Lysander walked over to the flashing yellow crystal and drove the knife deep through it. A flash of blinding yellow light was emitted, and the crystal that had started all this trouble broke cleanly in half. Morugan and his followers would never again be able to regenerate themselves, as vampires were able to do. Never again would they threaten the lives of the innocent.

VIII
Finally Free

"Anna!" Mr. Harper ran immediately to his motion-less daughter and took her in his arms. She was pale as death, and felt cold. "Oh my God, Anna." He hugged her tight.

Lysander looked on in silence. Grief flooded through him, but he did not dare to go closer, an intruder upon the sorrow of the man before him.

I am a disgrace, the vampire thought dully. *I lost my own family to those demons, and now I have taken this man's daughter from him. And all because I was too weak to fight their mind games. She was the only joy he had left. It should have been me, not her. Not Anna.*

He could stand the sight no longer, he turned to leave.

"Where are you going?" The question, echoing around the room, startled the vampire. Why was Anna's father speaking to him after what he had done?

"I'm leaving. She was better off never knowing me."

Then Mr. Harper said the strangest thing. "She wouldn't have blamed you. I don't blame you."

"Don't you realize what I have done?"

"I realize she was right to trust you. I realize that you risked your own life to save her. It was nothing less than I would have done myself."

"I loved her," the vampire said. "I never intended for your daughter to be hurt, I hope you understand that."

"I know." Mr. Harper stroked his daughter's wavy blond hair. "I know you didn't."

Here it was again, honest and unbidden forgiveness, just like his mother had offered when he had failed to save his sisters life. Just like Anna had offered when he had nearly taken hers. He swallowed hard.

"Anna." Tentatively he went over to them and took the girl's hand in his. "Oh, my darling." He closed his wind stung eyes for a moment and listened to her pulse, in stark contrast to his own motionless heart.

Wait a minute! *Pulse?!*

He listened more carefully. Yes. It was very weak, but it was there. He heard her breathing, barely audible. His eyes flew open.

"She's alive." He looked at her face. "Anna?"

"Are you sure?"

"Positive." Lysander looked around, as though not completely certain that they were alone. "We should go, there will be hunters swarming around here in no time at all." He stood and went for the door, and Mr. Harper followed carrying his daughter.

When they got back to the house Mr. Harper laid Anna carefully on the couch and pulled a blanket up around her to keep her warm, but the girl did not awaken.

"Come on, honey, wake up," he said desperately as he put a damp rag to her forehead to try and revive her. She shuddered, but remained unconscious.

Lysander looked on, thinking. He could try to heal her, but there were no guarantees that approach would work when she was in this state...

Why not? He owed it to them to at least try.

"I have an idea," he said finally.

"You can help her?"

"I can try. Nothing more." The vampire knelt at Anna's side and, placing his fingertips at her temples, began to mutter the same healing incantation he had used to mend the burns inflicted by the hunter. He focused solely on his love for Anna. His wish to save her filled him.

Mr. Harper watched, entranced. Could it work? Could the vampire really save his daughter? It seemed so absurd, but he felt nothing could surprise him anymore.

Finally Anna's eyes fluttered open, and she looked at her friend.

"Lysander." She propped herself up on her elbows.

"You're all right now," he told her. "You're home. Anna, I was so afraid I would lose you."

"*I* was afraid *I'd* lost *you*." Anna winced in pain; her head was aching fit to burst. "Ugh. I hate magic."

Lysander produced a small vial containing a solution of Lavender and Sage, and handed it to her. "Here."

Anna drank, and suddenly felt the pain leave her. "Thank you." She sank back on the pillow, feeling immense relief and exhaustion, and then looked over at her father. "Hi, Dad."

"My little girl." Mr. Harper leaned over and hugged his daughter. "Don't ever scare me like that again." There were tears in his eyes, even though he was smiling.

"Sorry." Anna grinned weakly.

"Look, Anna," Lysander faltered. "What happened tonight-I am so sorry. I was truly a beast."

"I told you before, you are not a beast." Anna reached out and laced her fingers between his, and the vampire grinned. "You came through when I needed you, like I knew you would. A beast wouldn't have saved my life twice in the same night, for God's sake. So, that other vampire's dead?"

"Yes. You helped me to triumph over him when he made me a prisoner of my own fury, and for that I will always be grateful to you."

"It was no trouble," Anna said brightly. "I kind of liked being able to stir-fry that creep Garrison anyway. How was I able to do that?"

"I'm not sure. I can only assume it was an inborn ability that had not manifested itself until now. Not everyone can summon a vampire, my dear girl."

"What happened to the crystal?"

"Destroyed," Lysander said simply. "I had to make sure that Morugan and his clan would never be able to return again."

"I suppose it was for the best," Anna replied thoughtfully. "But you-you won't ever be able to see the sun again. You'll be stuck with a lifetime of being a creature of the night."

"I've already told you, that doesn't matter to me. I'm free from Morugan for good now, and I was able to see my friend through before I leave. I am content."

"Leave?" Anna asked, her eyes going wide. "How? The vampire hunters will be crawling all over this city looking for you. How will you get past them?"

"Don't worry for me," he reassured her. "I'll find a way. What matters is I'm able to go where others need my help. I'll finally be able to make good on that promise I made to my little sister all those years ago. Besides, your father wouldn't like you being up this late anyway." He smiled, just slightly, but without cheer. It would hurt to leave.

"I see," Anna said. "I want you to be someplace safe now." And the exhausted girl's eyes closed once more.

Such a pure girl, Lysander thought. After being attacked twice and nearly losing her life, she was still most concerned for him.

Lysander leaned over and kissed her cheek so gently that she did not stir.

"She'll miss you," Mr. Harper said.

"It's better this way." Lysander took one last look at his friend, and then rose to his feet. The Sage would give her a peaceful sleep, and she would be protected with her father nearby. "She'll be safer without me around. Take good care of her."

"I certainly will." Mr. Harper sat by Anna's side, where he would remain throughout the night. "Thank you, my friend." But the vampire had departed, silent as a shadow.

The next day Anna took off from school to attend Jennifer's wake with her father. When it was her turn to go past the casket, she placed a blue Iris-Jennifer's favorite flower-on top.

"Best friends forever," she whispered, so no one could hear, and tears started streaming down her face. It just seemed too horrible to think that she would never see her friend again.

On the way home Anna looked silently out the window.

"Are you okay, honey?" Her father asked.

Anna turned back to him and nodded. "I am now that the people who did this to Jennifer are gone. Hey, Dad, I think I do want to go with you when you leave on Sunday after all."

"Why's that? I thought you said you liked it here."

"I did," said Anna thoughtfully. "But Jen's gone. I'm all alone now."

"You'll make new friends, Anna," Her father said. But she shook her head no.

"No, I belong with you, seeing the world. I've always known that deep down. Besides, there's no telling what you'll find in Moscow. There has to be someone who's ready for anything that might happen."

"You were very brave fighting those vampires," Mr. Harper said. "I was extremely proud, and I know your mother would have been, too. But it just doesn't seem like something a fourteen-year old should be doing."

"I really don't think I'll be in any less danger here."

"And what about school? It's only October, and you want to leave already?"

"I can be home schooled like I was before."

"Your Aunt is going to throw a fit," Mr. Harper sighed.

"That'll be a sight for sore eyes," Anna said cheerfully. A silence elapsed, and then she asked, "Do you think Lysander is safe where he is now?"

"With powers like his, I have no doubt about it."

"It's good that he's decided to go where he can help other people," Anna said. "I don't need him anymore." But there was sadness in her voice.

Mr. Harper said, "He won't forget you. He loved you more than you know."

Anna looked out the window and said nothing more. But instead of frowning she was smiling. It was a beautiful day, really. The sky was a robin's egg blue, and the trees were covered with new white blossoms.

Thank you, Lysander, She thought. *Thank you for giving me the opportunity to see another beautiful day. I understand what you mean now. Be safe, wherever you are.*

Blood Means Everything

Bucharest, Romania, 1875: Dr. Lysander Heistad, a young physician known for his aptitude and unwavering compassion, had never hesitated to put others before himself. So when he heard the last request of his beloved little sister as she lay ravaged by Typhoid Fever, he never intended to fail in fulfilling it. However, he also had not foreseen himself being the target of a horrifying monster out for blood.....

New York, New York, 1995: For more than a century Lysander Heistad`s only companions have been other vampires, who shun him for his refusal to drink human blood. Consumed by guilt over the death of his sister, he had believed himself doomed to an eternity of loneliness and regret. When he meets Anna Harper, a beautiful, lonely and fearless mortal who trusts him implicitly, he can hardly believe his good fortune. But as their newfound friendship grows, so does his struggle to protect her, not only from other vampires, but from himself.

About the Author

Michelle Lynn Tackes is from Watertown, Wisconsin, and is an English major at the University of Wisconsin Whitewater. She has always had an affinity for stories of the supernatural, and conceived the idea for a story about a friendly vampire three years ago on her birthday. {Which, coincidentally, is two weeks before Halloween!} She is a published poet, and is currently working on her second novel.